on track ...
Status Quo

the Frantic Four years

Richard James

SONICBOND

sonicbondpublishing.com

Sonicbond Publishing Limited

www.sonicbondpublishing.co.uk

Email: info@sonicbondpublishing.co.uk

First Published in the United Kingdom 2021

First Published in the United States 2021

British Library Cataloguing in Publication Data:

A Catalogue record for this book is available from the British Library

Typeset in ITC Garamond & ITC Avant Garde

Printed and bound in England

Graphic design and typesetting: Full Moon Media

on track ...

Status Quo

the Frantic Four years

Richard James

sonicbondpublishing.com

Would you like to write for Sonicbond Publishing?

We are mainly a music publisher, but we also occasionally publish in other genres including film and television. At Sonicbond Publishing we are always on the look-out for authors, particularly for our two main series, On Track and Decades.

Mixing fact with in depth analysis, the On Track series examines the entire recorded work of a particular musical artist or group. All genres are considered from easy listening and jazz to 60s soul to 90s pop, via rock and metal.

The Decades series singles out a particular decade in an artist or group's history and focuses on that decade in more detail than may be allowed in the On Track series.

While professional writing experience would, of course, be an advantage, the most important qualification is to have real enthusiasm and knowledge of your subject. First-time authors are welcomed, but the ability to write well in English is essential.

Sonicbond Publishing has distribution throughout Europe and North America, and all our books are also published in E-book form. Authors will be paid a royalty based on sales of their book. Further details about our books are available from www.sonicbondpublishing.com. To contact us, complete the contact form there or email info@sonicbondpublishing.co.uk

Acknowledgements

Alison James – for patience over and above
that is required by marital vows.

Mike Rawsthorne – the Parfitt to my Rossi, and for
reading everything I write and sometimes laughing.

Ralph Snowden – for knowing more about
motorbikes than I ever will.

on track ...

Status Quo

Contents

'How Are You Then? Alright?'

When he heard that I was writing a book reviewing the songs of Status Quo a good friend of mine quipped, 'Does that mean you can't use words with more than three syllables?' This, for him, is quite funny. But all credit to Graham for his contribution; he has patiently endured, for many years, my endless jibes regarding his fascination with the prog-rock group Marillion, the diet version of Genesis.

Graham, like many, many others before him, has unwittingly bought into the lazy stereotyping of Quo by a music media that seemed set on savaging them even before they had their hit single breakthrough, 'Paper Plane', in 1972. During the first half of the Seventies, Quo produced a stream of inventive, complex blues rock songs which broke the genre's mould. The second half of the decade, and the early 1980s, saw increasing commercialisation set in to their core sound with some excellent, but mostly dubious, results.

But make no mistake. Quo were innovators, and deserve an appreciation beyond the default setting of 'moronic three-chord wonders'. What the hard-of-thinking critics are actually attacking is a *genre*. Take rock and roll, or blues, or country music. Artists composing in these styles all rely heavily upon three chords (tonic, sub-dominant, and dominant seventh, or I, IV and V as they can also be referred to). What Quo did worked extremely well within their chosen style, whether playing it straight (think 'Caroline') or making it shuffle ('Whatever You Want'). They were as successful as they were creative and influential.

Chart conquest, both with singles and albums, and thousands of gigs in front of incredibly loyal audiences defined them as a 'People's Band', not beholden to the fleeting nature of musical fashion. Their 'look' (tee-shirts, jeans, and trainers) was just a representation of what they truly were, a working class band from South London. They played the music they loved to fans who were just like them. Despite their phenomenal, and virtually unmatched, success, Quo are rarely thought of in the same light as other major bands of the era (Black Sabbath, Queen, Led Zeppelin, Deep Purple *et al*). Quo made a unique and highly significant contribution to rock music, and yet the critic's arrows still managed to pierce the public consciousness more effectively.

It seemed that whilst the work and legacy of other giants of the period was deserving of serious journalistic approval, the press also needed a whipping boy, a scapegoat band, if you will. And Quo, with their unpretentious music and denim-led look, provided the perfect target. From the 1980s onwards, the critics' comments were on the money. Today the band is a British institution, playing pop-based boogie with a highly commercial edge to an audience that spans entire generations of families. In the Seventies, they were, most definitely, something special.

Anyhoo, Graham's version of a joke gave me an idea. How many songs by the 'Frantic Four' actually consist of *just three chords?* What is the average number of chords per song? Which song has the highest total? And which the lowest? I thought an analysis of the default insult could be an interesting exercise. So, armed with a Telecaster (what else?), an amplifier set to squirrel-bothering volumes, and a smattering of musical knowledge, I set to work. Each song review includes a chord count, and the final chapter of this book, 'The End Of This Road', contains the surprising conclusions.

One response to the eternal jibe is, of course, 'Who cares? It's great music'. This was the fans' standpoint whenever confronted with the comment. Quo, and their music, mattered to them; a music critic's opinion (be they a school friend, drinking buddy, or a music journalist) did not. But this stance implicitly assumes the critic to be correct. As this vital musicologist research will prove, this is *not the case*. Quo found their sound, stuck to their goals, worked incredibly hard, and deserved all the acclaim a grateful audience could shower on them. Another regular criticism was that they wrote 'meaningless songs'. Again, the important point is missed; rock records tend to make their impact through the music rather than the lyrics. We tend to notice the words more once we've absorbed the sounds. And Quo's music had the power to move us.

Just to clarify, when I write about a 'chord', I am referring to a group of notes played simultaneously. This is not the same as a 'riff' which is a short, oft-repeated sequence of individual notes. In Quo-land, an example of a riff would be the four-note descending sequence introduction to 'Paper Plane', followed by a mixture of A5 and A6 chords. Whilst A5 and A6 are subtly different chords, I file them together under the single tonality of A major, or 'one chord'. Or, as a slightly longer example, take the introduction to 'Backwater; the first twenty seconds are a riff, and underpinning this when the phrases are repeated is a chord progression.

My introduction to Quo was via the three-track live EP, featuring 'Roll Over Lay Down', 'Gerdundula', and 'Junior's Wailing' released in May 1975. I just *loved* the sound the band made, and the first album I bought was *On The Level*, later that year. The first gig I saw was Quo at the now-defunct Granby Halls in Leicester on the *Rocking All Over The World* tour in December 1977. It was a fantastic night. My ears rang for the next three days. I didn't care. Quo became my 'first love' in a lengthy list of long term relationships with rock music.

The origins of the band go back to school days. Francis Rossi and Alan Lancaster met at Sedgehill Comprehensive School in Beckenham, South London, playing in the School orchestra as an excuse to avoid lessons. Later they formed a band with Jess Jaworski, an organ player, and drummer Barry Smith calling themselves The Paladins. This was quickly changed to The Scorpions and soon, they became The Spectres. Legend has it that their first gig was at the Samuel Jones Sports Club in Dulwich in May 1962.

Rehearsals moved out of parent's houses to the nearby Territorial Army barracks, where a greater noise could be made. This was also used by the local Air Training Corps, and another group, The Cadets, also practised there whose drummer, John Coghlan was quickly persuaded to join The Spectres. Jaworski left the group to continue his school studies, his replacement being Roy Lynes. The band's part-time manager, Pat Barlow, organised some gigs and managed to land the group a Summer Season contract at Butlins in Minehead, Somerset, in 1965. This was also where Rick Parfitt, working under the name of Ricky Harrison, was appearing as part of a cabaret trio, 'The Highlights', with singing twin-sisters Jean and Gloria Harrison. It was at Butlins that Rossi and Parfitt struck up a friendship.

The Spectres recorded a demo tape which Barlow used to secure a record deal with Piccadilly Records, a subsidiary of Pye Records. Their debut single, a cover of Shirley Bassey's 'I Who Have Nothing', was released in September 1966, and flopped. 'Hurdy Gurdy Man', an early writing credit for Alan Lancaster (November 1966), and 'We Ain't Got Nothing Yet' (February 1967), continued the trend. The band threw the dice again with a name change, hoping to court attention, and became 'The Traffic Jam'.

As the saying goes, there's no such thing as bad publicity. Another single, 'Almost But Not Quite There' (June 1967), was banned by the BBC for the innuendos in Rossi's lyrics. Furthermore, Steve Winwood, fresh from The Spencer Davis Group, had a new band, Traffic, who had scored a hit with 'Paper Sun' in May 1967. He didn't care for a similarly titled band being in the public eye, which resulted in another name change, this time to 'The Status Quo'.

The continuing persistence of Barlow, and Pye's 'in-house' producer John Schroeder, together with the addition of Rick Parfitt, originally recruited to the band for his singing ability rather than as a guitar player, eventually began to bear fruit. A breakthrough occurred when the Rossi penned, psychedelia-influenced single 'Pictures Of Matchstick Men' became a hit in January 1968, reaching number seven in the charts. Rossi admitted to some confusion over the band's identity and musical direction at the time in the 2014 documentary film *Hello Quo!*

When we broke we were a rock band with a soul set and a psychedelic single. I didn't even know what psychedelic meant … I was copying things.

However, the follow-up, 'Black Veils Of Melancholy' (March 1968) a virtual facsimile of 'Matchstick Men', failed spectacularly. The band's third single, a zingy, rhythmic cover of 'Ice In The Sun' (July 1968), returned them to the charts reaching number eight. Temporary teen-pop stardom seemed to be the band's future, but it wasn't a future they desired.

In September 1968, the album, *Picturesque Matchstickable Messages From The Status Quo,* was released, and this too failed to chart. A dreadful title but a terrific score in 'Scrabble', the album was a compilation of previously released singles and B sides. It lasts 35 minutes (but *feels* much longer), and, if you were of an unkind nature, you would say it's the aural equivalent of being water-boarded. A better angel could view the lightweight material as being typical of the pop music of the period. But there was too much evidence of pastiche, or slavish impersonation, of similar music produced by The Beatles, The Kinks, and others; bands who not only did it first but did it better. The track listing was:

'Black Veils Of Melancholy' (Rossi)
'When My Mind Is Not Live' (Rossi/Parfitt)
'Ice In The Sun' (Wilde/Scott)
'Elizabeth Dreams' (Wilde/Scott)
'Gentleman Joe's Sidewalk Café' (Young)
'Paradise Flat' (Wilde/Scott)
'Technicolor Dreams' (King)
'Spicks And Specks' (Gibb)
'Sheila' (Roe)
'Sunny Cellophane Skies' (Lancaster)
'Green Tambourine' (Leka/Pinz)
'Pictures Of Matchstick Men' (Rossi)

Almost exactly a year later, Quo's second album, *Spare Parts*, was issued. By now, the 'The' had been dropped from the band's title. There had been a brief flirtation with the shortening of the name still further to S.Quo (hoping to mirror the success of Marc Bolan's T Rex); an idea which was wisely discarded. Despite such revolutionary steps the band's chart-dodging trend continued. Pye Records was part of the problem; they focused on hit singles, with albums being seen as a less important by-product. Their roster of artists was distinctly 'Middle of the Road', a 'crooner's corner' if you like, and they weren't a good fit for the ambitious Quo, who were moving with the current thinking. Rock music was becoming serious, the band should look serious, and they wanted to release a serious rock album

    Spare Parts, whilst better than its predecessor, still wasn't representative of where Quo wanted to be. The album was neither a collection of commercial hits nor a cool, 'muso experience'. The songs were poppy, sometimes overly sentimental, and the inclusion of string and brass arrangements did nothing to suggest what lay beneath the façade of the band's Carnaby Street clothing. The track listing was:

'Face Without A Soul' (Rossi/Parfitt)
'You're Just What I Was Looking For Today' (Goffin/King)
'Are You Growing Tired Of My Love' (King)
'Antique Angelique' (Lancaster/Young)
'So Ends Another Life' (Lancaster)
'Poor Old Man' (Rossi/Parfitt)
'Mr Mind Detector' (King)
'The Clown' (Lancaster/Lynes/ Young)

'Velvet Curtains' (King)
'Little Miss Nothing' (Rossi/Parfitt)
'When I Awake' (Lancaster/Young)
'Nothing At All' (Lancaster/Lynes/Young)

Despite this, the band's live shows were always a high energy rock and roll event. Quo had been working with the twelve-bar groove with which they would become synonymous from their earliest gigs, as evidenced by 'Bloodhound', an energetic track which appeared on the four-disc set *'Live At The BBC'* released in 2010. They regularly performed covers of rock and roll songs which made the transition into what they would become, an easy and natural one.

'Are You Growing Tired Of My Love' was the only single released from *'Spare Parts'*, and managed to scrape to 46 in the charts in April 1969. Quo's final assault on the Sixties was a cover of The Everly Brothers' 'The Price Of Love' in September 1969. Whilst this was notable for the first appearance of Bob Young's harmonica playing, even this wasn't enough to help it chart. Young had been employed as a roadie, and would soon begin to develop as a lyricist with significant results.

As the new decade dawned, Quo's fortunes weren't looking healthy. Psychedelic tinged pop success wasn't their true leaning, time was moving on, and Pye Records were losing faith in their signing. The band dispensed with the brightly coloured garb of the late Sixties in favour of the 'day-wear', faded, scruffy denims. Hair was grown fashionably long, and tee-shirts and jeans were the order of the day and night. Record sales and bookings were in what looked like a permanent decline. But all was not lost. In *Status Quo – The Official 40th Anniversary Edition* (2006) Parfitt recalls an incident in early 1970 which provided both inspiration and direction for the band:

Me and Francis were out at this club in Germany, we were sort of just sitting there drunk and we saw this couple dancing to the Doors' 'Roadhouse Blues', it had this infectious shuffle beat and the way they were moving their bodies, they were really silky and really smooth – it kind of turned us on. And that's largely responsible for why we do so many of these shuffle rhythms, it turns us on. We like it and it's become our trademark, and all that because we were getting drunk and watching this couple dance in that soppy little club.

Another significant event occurred in April 1970 at a gig in South London, as Rossi recalled in *The Status Quo Autobiography* (2004);

The first real step forward to becoming the band we are now, came unexpectedly one night when we simply decided to go on stage in our normal street wear. We were appearing at the Castle Pub in Tooting supporting Mott The Hoople, and we just couldn't be bothered to put all the clobber on and go through the same routine again. So we went on as we were, in jeans and tee-shirts, and started belting out some of the blues shuffles that we had been noodling around with at sound-check. I kept waiting for someone to come on and tell us to stop messing about and get back to the proper stuff, nobody came and we ended up going down a storm.

Fate lent a hand when Colin Johnson became their agent and, within a year, manager. Johnson saw potential in the music that Quo wanted to play, and was determined to spread the word far and wide. He insisted that the band should gig anywhere and everywhere they could. Johnson also booked them into Pye Studios in London to record a new single which was more representative of their natural rocking style.

In March 1970, 'Down The Dustpipe' appeared, which is the opening chapter in the 'true' Quo story. Thanks to word-of-mouth recommendation from a small but growing base of hardcore fans, and relentless gigging, the song would eventually reach number 12 in the charts. This was followed by 'In My Chair', the first Rossi/Young composition, in October 1970, which went to number 21. In August 1970, the band's third album, the radically different sounding *Ma Kelly's Greasy Spoon,* fundamentally the first 'real' Quo album, was released, and it was from here the band's fortunes finally began to change. The sobriquet 'The Frantic Four' was borne out of the band's energetic stage performances, as Rossi surmised in *Status Quo – The Authorised Biography* (1979):

> We'd always had this thing where we rocked a bit on stage. You couldn't help it really. And you've got to remember we were brought up on playing all that Chuck Berry stuff we're meant to have ripped off. Underneath, it was always natural, always there. It was expected that we'd move a bit. Even as early as 1969, they'd described us 'as moving across the stage like a pack of hungry panthers'.

This book focuses on the period 1970-84 when, in my opinion, Quo were, mostly, at their best. I have not reviewed the band's first two albums as that music bears no relation to what emerged during the Seventies. From the start of the decade, Quo progressed rapidly to a peak with the all-conquering *Blue For You* in 1976. A double live album proved to be an apex for the band, with subsequent releases, whilst still sporadically powerful, showing some unwelcome changes, either in production, arrangements, or song-writing. Sometimes all three elements would combine to create a perfect storm of disappointment.

By 1982 the 'Frantic Four' had shrunk to three with the departure of John Coghlan, and Alan Lancaster's subsequent exit three years later led to the effective demise of the band. A 'final' appearance as opening act at 'Live Aid' in July 1985 threw Quo back into the public spotlight. By this time, inter-band relations were at such a low point that the original line-up, what was left of it, couldn't, wouldn't, and didn't want to continue.

Of course, Rossi and Parfitt revived the name in 1986 and continued for the next four decades as, fundamentally, a good time pop-boogie band. In the penultimate chapter of this book I offer an abridged overview of their substantial output; not because I think it's any good (most of it just isn't), but as an acknowledgement of the continuity of the brand.

But Quo made their name and established their true legacy in the 1970s, and this book is both a celebration and a critique of that. The early significant musical achievements are too easily overshadowed by their commercial drift in the late 1970s and early 1980s, which turned into an tsunami following the 1986 reinvention. By that time, the critics had a point, but before then, they were way, way off base.

Buckle up Graham, see you in 150 songs' time…

Ma Kelly's Greasy Spoon

Personnel:
Francis Rossi: lead guitar and vocals
Rick Parfitt: guitar and vocals
Alan Lancaster: bass and vocals
Roy Lynes: organ
John Coghlan: drums
Guest musician: Bob Young: harmonica
Produced by John Schroeder
Recorded at Pye Records, London
Released on 28 August 1970

As the 1960s album charts had ignored Status Quo, and, more importantly for their record label, the hit singles had dried up, Pye Records were less and less bothered about the fate of the band. As Parfitt said in a BBC radio interview in July 1979:

> We were being told what to do then because in those days we were very young, and somebody said 'Right, you're gonna be pop stars lads', and we went 'Yeah, great, mister, fantastic', and he said 'You'll wear this, and you will play this' and we were forced to conform. Then came a time when we were a bit sick of it, and we were going down like a steel balloon in the ballrooms. So we literally came off the road and just sort of started wearing the denim quite naturally.

In *Hello Quo!,* he added:

> And we were missing what we were really, you know, which was jeans. We liked jeans and pumps and tee-shirts, and that's really kind of how we saw the band.

The transition from pop group to rock band is at its most stark with the cover of the new album. There are no photographs of the band. This reticence, whether deliberate or not, certainly distanced Quo from their former, brightly lit, poppy persona. The 1970s band was clearly going to be a very different animal. The mood of *Ma Kelly's...* is sombre and, to a degree, at odds with the music. On the front cover is a bored-looking middle-aged lady with an (unlit) cigarette in her mouth. She may be the owner, or possibly a waitress at a 'Greasy Spoon', the colloquial term for the type of establishment where paying as little as possible for food trumps other concerns, like hygiene or comfort. She is the centre of attention. The rear of the sleeve has a separate photo of a café table, replete with an old cup of coffee, a salt cellar, a bottle of tomato ketchup, and an upright piece of paper listing the song titles. Also included on the side is some nonsense 'poetry' by Bob Young;

S.Quo. Labelled? Hey Mable, no label. Francis nuff ric cog lib. Working their wot off? Struggle. What isn't who isn't. Where are you? Hyde and seek. They can see you. Want to feel you. Inky fingers words saying. Tui! Tui! Moths to butterflies. Can't be done. Poop! It's done. And thank Christ for yesterday.

Yeah. Right. On. Man.
In his 2019 book *I Talk Too Much* Rossi explained the idea behind the downbeat cover:

Ma Kelly's Greasy Spoon (was) a reference to the types of places we found ourselves eating in while we were on the road, which we were constantly in those days. Those places all seemed to be run by the same stone-faced middle-aged woman with a cigarette butt dangling from her lips, hence the 'greasy' sepia picture on the front of the album sleeve. I'm not sure if we meant this, but looking at the picture now, it's also quite a good metaphor for the music evolution we were undergoing – from pop dandies to down-and-dirty blues rockers.

Quo knew what they wanted to play and how they wanted to play it. In *Hello Quo!* Lancaster said of the album:

Although it was a little bit kind of wonky ... there's some pretty good stuff on there.

And it was during their relentless gigging schedule that the band would write 'some pretty good stuff' and try it out at gigs. If the reaction was positive, the song might make it onto an album. Quo weren't alone in this approach; the idea of going into a recording studio to write material was not an economic way of working for struggling artists. Songs were written on the road and recorded at a later stage. For example, 'Caroline' was played on the tour for *Piledriver* before it made its appearance on *Hello!*, and 'Big Fat Mama' was similarly bludgeoning audiences around the time of *Dog Of Two Head* before being released on the band's first album for their new label, Vertigo.

This technique was also a secret weapon in fending off the critics' attacks. The fans experienced the songs live before the reviewers heard the record and the expanding fan-base 'word-of-mouth' overrode anything a music journalist could convey by way of persuasion. This by-passing of the traditional formula meant that the 'new' band's first single, 'Down The Dustpipe', was a chart success despite a lack of radio airplay, or support from DJs. Quo sold records on the basis of their many live gigs and growing reputation. Rossi acknowledged this in an interview with *Melody Maker* in November 1975:

This band has not existed by selling product and then going out and playing it. It's the other way with Quo. We sell so many albums because we play so much on the road. Kids hear us and then go and buy the albums.

Ma Kelly's... was the first opportunity for the record-buying public to savour the band's new sound. Essentially their first 'serious rock' album was an audio diary of their live set at the turn of the decade, comprising a mix of covers and original compositions. However *Ma Kelly's...* is nevertheless still an important stepping stone between the pop sensibilities of their first two long-players and where the band were headed.

Peculiarly the original vinyl release excluded 'Down The Dustpipe'. The 2003 CD re-issue features 'Down The Dustpipe', and the post-album single 'In My Chair', together with alternate versions of some of the album's tracks. Also included is a new song, 'Gerdundula', which had been the B-side to 'In My Chair', and had been re-recorded for possible inclusion on the album. No singles from the album itself were issued, although 'Shy Fly' was briefly considered.

Ma Kelly's... was the last album to feature Roy Lynes, the keyboard player with the haunted look of a man not allowed within 100 metres of his son's school. Lynes noted the band's guitar-driven rock direction and decided his own contribution was not fitting in sufficiently. He left prior to the recording of 'In My Chair', with his departure only helping to tighten Quo as a musical unit. Another interesting facet of the release is the emergence of Rossi and Young as a song-writing team; they contributed four tracks, whilst Lancaster provided three of the album's heavier numbers.

I have a lot of affection for *Ma Kelly's...*. The 'Quo Shuffle', even in its early stages, is persuasively effective on tracks like 'Spinning Wheel Blues' and 'Junior's Wailing'. There is plenty of light and shade with the softer tracks, 'Everything' and 'Lakky Lady', in-between the burgeoning heaviness of 'Daughter' and 'Need Your Love'. Equally, there is melodic skill in 'Shy Fly' and '(April), Spring, Summer, and Wednesdays', which show that the now 'Frantic Four' were establishing their true range and sound, with their collective eyes very much set on the future.

Ma Kelly's... emphasised that Quo's Sixties past was behind them and that their 'new direction' was heartfelt and authentic. And this newfound musical freedom, despite the misgivings of Pye Records, saw them carve out a place in the evolving heavy rock music scene, which they would dominate for the next ten years. The music on *Ma Kelly's...* is exciting, varied, different, inspired, well written and arranged, and a genuine indicator of what was to come.

'Spinning Wheel Blues' (Rossi/Young) Duration: 3.17 Chord Count: 3

Setting aside 'Down The Dustpipe' temporarily, the opening song of the new era lays down many pointers to the band's future success. Coghlan's rock-solid drumming and Lancaster's throbbing bass underpin Rossi's reedy vocals in this up-tempo, twelve-bar blues shuffle ode to the perils of gambling. 'Spinning Wheel Blues' replicates the archetypal low mood associated with the blues.

A four-bar introduction with Rossi's distorted lead fills prominent and Parfitt's rhythm work well down in the mix, is followed by two verses, the second of which adds harmony vocals and some honky-tonk piano. The first guitar solo, with keyboards supporting in the background, is split into two twelve-bar sequences. The third verse returns to the sparser texture of the first verse, with the keyboards and harmony vocals rejoining for the final verse.

Bob Young adds a harmonica solo over the final instrumental section which is a single play-through of the twelve-bar chord progression. The band come to a sudden stop on the first beat of the tenth bar of the next section leaving room for a brief lead guitar flourish before the music fades on a repeated strummed G7 chord, as Coghlan rolls around his kit with abandon.

'Daughter' (Lancaster) Duration: 2.59 Chord Count: 4

Lancaster's composition highlights his preferred style of song writing. 'Daughter' is a relentlessly heavy, riff-driven foot-tapper. The track is based around a C seventh chord for the three verses before modulating into B flat for the chorus ('Daughter, can you have sons for yourself'?), where vocal harmonies add a degree of quality. There is an impressive chromatic descending scale into a repeat of this refrain which brings the music back into its original driving groove.

The lyrics are indistinct due to the over-application of reverb, and the short delay added to the vocals, another link (if not a particularly strong one) to the band's former psychedelic dalliances. After the second chorus and a repeat of the eight-bar introduction, Lynes throws in a fine organ solo, which he then reprises after the third verse and chorus as the song chugs away happily to a fade.

'Everything' (Rossi/Parfitt) Duration: 2.34 Chord Count: 12

'Everything' is an astonishing handbrake turn of a song and should be heard by everyone who thought that the new Quo was only about grinding riffs and listener-flattening heaviness. Musically, this sparse ballad features two acoustic guitars, (one nylon strung, one steel strung), together with a cello, played by an uncredited musician, producing some beautiful interweaving melody lines amongst the steady guitar arpeggios.

Lyrically 'Everything' is even more of a surprise as the song deals with a girl losing her virginity, told from the male perspective. Sung by Parfitt with a restrained tone, there is a sense of introspection to this ballad, which is well encapsulated in the coda lyrics 'And who knows what it'll mean'. On subsequent albums, the curtain would sometimes be lifted on Parfitt's image as the quintessential hard rock'n'roller, and this gentle song is the first example.

Musically the rise and fall in the underlying chord progression neatly parallels the anticipation and then sad reality of the words. 'Everything' is closer to the style of composition made popular by singer-songwriters of the period, rather than a pop style of music. Quo offer up an artistic, evocative piece as a contrast to what they are also capable of and, as such, it is an effective ear-opener to new fans.

'Shy Fly' (Rossi/Young) Duration: 3.46 Chord Count: 4

And the variety keeps coming. 'Shy Fly' is a bright, optimistic-sounding pop-rock song with a solid, driving rhythm, decorative bluesy guitar fills, and sly vocals. But there's more lurking beneath the surface with a clever syncopated twist at the end of the introduction where the music moves into a single bar of 2/4 time before setting up Rossi's melodic lead phrases, which intersperse the lyrics. Lynes's organ is prominent, and it's good to hear Parfitt's relentless rhythm work sounding more front and centre in the mix.

Lyrically obscure, Young's words concern a relationship between a tiger and a fly. Perhaps there was a spider shortage at the time. No doubt it meant something to him. The song is saved, however, by its strong central vocal melody, with effective harmonies in the chorus and a sense of *joie de vivre* throughout the performance.

'(April), Spring, Summer, and Wednesdays' (Rossi/Young) Duration: 4.10 Chord Count: 9

This curiously titled, funky little groover is another change of musical direction; there is no hint of twelve-bar blues or up-tempo boogie to be found here. Built around a laid back electric guitar riff with bass and drums joining in, the verse grooves along merrily with Rossi's giving distinctive voice to Young's, let's be kind, occasionally contradictory words, 'I can't leave, but I won't stay here, if I stay, I still won't be here'. Yeah. Right. On. Man. Again.

The chorus sound is heavier with the addition of a weighty rhythm guitar before reaching the sing-a-long refrain at 0.44. Lyrically the song has a dark theme; a woman seems to be exerting a metaphysical power over a man's mind, and this mood is reinforced by the hypnotic feel of the underlying music.

The second verse, chorus and refrain follow the same sonic pattern until the instrumental section at 2.12, which comprises an unusual and yet still melodic chord progression. There is no guitar or keyboard solo. The sequence is interspersed with a two beats' rest before reverting to the introduction, which precedes the third verse, chorus and refrain, which are reruns of the first versions. The chord instrumental returns at 3.31 for the song's coda and the track is rounded off with repeated D and C major chords before some studio trickery manipulates the pitch of a distorted guitar feedback to its close.

'(April), Spring, Summer, and Wednesdays' shows that, even in this early stage of their development, Quo were more than capable of writing intricate, innovative music grounded in blues rock. The song would be a surprising and welcome addition to the set list for the 'Frantic Four' reunion tours in 2013 and 2014.

'Junior's Wailing' (White/Pugh) Duration: 3.32 Chord Count: 6

We're back to the land of the heavy shuffle with Lancaster taking the vocals on the song first released by Steamhammer in 1969. As the album's first cover version, it fares well and would be a regular gig opener up to and including the release of the double live album, *Live* in 1977.

As with 'Daughter', the studio treatment of Lancaster's voice in the heavier aspects of the song does him no favours. The Quo version has a meatier sound than the original, is at a slightly slower tempo, and is sonically less busy. After Rossi's convincing solo and a third verse, 'Junior's Wailing' drops in volume for two verses, the second being more restrained than the first. Lynes is absent from the mix which is to the song's benefit, and Rossi finishes proceedings off with another biting, melodic solo, and a surprisingly jazz-like ending of three ninth chords.

'Lakky Lady' (Rossi/Parfitt) Duration: 3.12 Chord Count: 7

The seventh song of the album continues the pleasing trend of variation. 'Lakky Lady' opens with some strummed acoustic guitar chords and a snippet of quiet conversation before a vigorous chord progression starts up. This is quickly joined by drums, organ, and, erm, bongos, in an enthusiastic, acoustic-pop track. 'Lakky' is slang for a lady who, how to put this, is keen to please, and the lyrics are less than complimentary about her at times. Rossi does, however, confess to loving her, 'and I need that woman so'. His mid-song solo features some well-phrased harmony lines amongst the bluesy phrases. This reinforces my long-held belief that he is a vastly under-rated lead guitarist, whose solos always rely upon melodic content rather than out and out flash playing.

'Need Your Love' (Rossi/Young) Duration: 4.45 Chord Count: 4

A heavy horse that sounds like it has escaped from the Lancaster stable, 'Need Your Love' is a relentless bruiser of a track which is really two satisfying songs in one.

The slower first half is based around a fluid riff involving the minor 2nd and flattened 3rd of the A minor scale. This gives the music a dark, intense feel, although the verse vocal melody is in the parallel key of A major. Again too much reverb has the effect of submerging Rossi's vocals, but the song wins out with its drive and powerfully tight rhythmic backbone.

At 2.06, the four-to-the-floor beat shifts gears into a 12/8 shuffle rhythm for the second part of the number. Here Rossi's guitar fills around Parfitt's vocals don't work so well, and the music comes to an abrupt halt at 3.30 before resuming the first section of the song. In the quick fade, we hear some rapid bass gymnastics from Lancaster.

'Lazy Poker Blues' (Green/Adams) Duration: 3.38 Chord Count: 3

This is the album's second cover, the song first being recorded by Fleetwood Mac in 1968. Unlike the original, which faded in and maintained a steady shuffle tempo throughout, Quo's version begins with a slow count into a heavy blues at a steady mid-paced tempo. Forty-seven seconds later, it lurches abruptly into double-time, with Lynes providing keyboard support behind Rossi's occasional fills. Parfitt's vocal performance sounds like the melody's range is, at times, a struggle for him.

Despite its title, 'Lazy Poker Blues' is not concerned with the benefits of maintaining a coal fire in cold weather. Rossi's solos are restrained and appropriately bluesy against the strong rhythmic backing, and bear similarities to Peter Green's tasteful, spacious fills. At the close, there is the bizarre sound effect of some running footsteps and what sounds like a laughing children's toy. No doubt it was very funny at the time.

'Is It Really Me?' (Lancaster) Duration: 2.47 Chord Count: 5
The pairing of 'Is It Really Me?' and 'Gotta Go Home' as a final lengthy piece presages the development of 'end of album' epics like 'Roadhouse Blues', 'Forty Five Hundred Times', 'Slow Train', and, to lesser extents, 'Mystery Song', and 'Breaking Away'.

Based around a simplistic pentatonic riff, 'Is It Really Me?' is another heavy rocker where Parfitt takes the lead vocals. A steady, driving rhythm under the verse gives way to a more melodic chorus, with vocal harmonies and sustained organ adding to the texture. At 1.48, a creative new section occurs; staccato phrases are played under the plaintive vocal tone, which moves into the chorus chord sequence without the words. There is a brief reprise of the chorus until an abrupt change of rhythm into 12/8 time as the song morphs into....

'Gotta Go Home' (Lancaster) Duration: 6.48 Chord Count: 3
'Gotta Go Home' is fundamentally 'Is It Really Me?' with a different rhythm, a faster tempo, new lyrics, and less invention. From 3.40, a lengthy instrumental section sets forth with Rossi savaging his Telecaster, whilst Lynes provides a soporific organ ostinato in the background. A second lead guitar part offers contrasting phrases until the second verse kicks in at 5.40.

Following the second chorus, we're into an indulgent solo section where improvisation rather than inspiration seems to have been the priority. At 8.31, a distorted Celtic style melody enters the fray, providing some interest, and Lynes, clearly boring even himself by now, starts attacking his keyboard with some ferocity as the track fades away. There is another curious end of track footnote with Parfitt intoning 'This is Status Quo saying…' before lurching into a Monty Python-esque voice 'Thank you-ou-ou'

Non-Album Tracks
'Down The Dustpipe' (Groszmann) Duration: 2.06 Chord Count: 6
Rossi commented in his autobiography on one of several turning points for Quo in the early stages of their transformation:

What I loved about 'Down The Dustpipe', which I had only just cottoned onto, was that it incorporated that fabulous Italian shuffle, only amped up and given a bit more whizz-bang. It just came so naturally to me, that perfect marriage of pop and blues, and to the rest of the band. At the time, there was a question mark over whether Pye would pay for us to make another album, but they were happy for us to record 'Down The Dustpipe' as a one-off single. I'm guessing the thinking was probably, well, if this isn't a hit, we'll just drop the band from the label. There was certainly no over-egging the pudding in the studio. We just went in and played it as we would live, more or less, with John Schroeder pushing the buttons.

Although based around the same twelve-bar structure as 'Spinning Wheel Blues', 'Down The Dustpipe' is a far more optimistic song as a result of the melodic line of the vocals. In the former the melody descends a considerable distance (the interval between 'spent' and 'night' is an inverted fifth). With 'Down The Dustpipe', the melody starts on the major third interval, rises from that to a perfect fifth, and then returns to it, immediately giving the music an uplifting feel.

Released as a single in March 1970, this cover version of the song originally recorded by Man is a brisk shuffle that powers along from Coghlan's single drum stab to the fade a mere two minutes later. The introduction, like the instrumental section after the third verse, benefits from Young's effective harmonica contribution, and Lynes's piano adds colour from the second verse onwards. Following Young's solo, the fourth verse reprises the second verse, which is repeated again as the music modulates up a semitone and quickly fades away. The B-side of the single was 'Face Without A Soul', an overly busy, attention-dodging, Rossi/Parfitt composition taken from *'Spare Parts'*.

'In My Chair' (Rossi/Young) Duration: 3.13 Chord Count: 4

Following the relative success of *Ma Kelly's...*, Pye allowed the band to go into the studio again. The result was 'In My Chair', another shuffling number, albeit at a slower tempo, which is very much a showcase for Rossi's talents. Whether it is his laconic delivery of Young's frankly downright weird words, or his melodic guitar solos, the lead guitarist is the focus of attention.

It seems that, lyrically at least, the band hadn't completely lost touch with their recently jettisoned psychedelic past. Take your pick from 'We ran along walking across the rooftops in my chair', 'Had a car in my pocket and we started moving', or 'My teeth were laughing now, we couldn't stop smiling'. 'In My Chair' is a confusing collision of two different worlds, but, strangely, it works.

The 1970s witnessed the birth and subsequent fan elevation of the 'Guitar God', with early heroes including Eric Clapton, Jimmy Page, and Tony Iommi. It is a credit to Quo's arranging skills that where the instrumental could have become Rossi's show-off moment, he keeps his contribution closely linked to the song's chord progression, using a combination of double stops and bluesy fills. This deviation from the fretboard fashion of the time further emphasised the fact that Quo saw themselves as a single unit, no one player being more, or less, important than any other.

Critics would single out 'On The Road Again' by Canned Heat, released in 1967, as an obvious comparison. There are similarities, although Quo's song dispenses with any pseudo-Indian drone instrumentation. Equally, Canned Heat employed a harmonica extensively, whilst 'In My Chair' features neither Young, nor the keyboard talents of Lynes. The vocal styling and overall laid back feel are the only real reference points between the two songs.

'Gerdundula' (Manston/James) Duration: 3.19 Chord Count: 5

This was the atypical B-side to 'In My Chair', and it's another wet fish to the face for the 'all their songs sound the same' brigade. 'Gerdundula' is built around a jaunty, folk style guitar riff with Lancaster playing acoustic guitar, and Coghlan banging a mean bongo. The track not only doesn't sound like Quo, it barely sounds like anybody else. There are some traces of early Steeleye Span and Horslips in the largely traditional instrument arrangement, and it's this absence of direct influences which makes the composition so intriguing. Only Rossi's distinctive vocal style, here in a relatively gentle acoustic setting, could give the game away as to who was performing the song.

Despite the writing credits, 'Gerdundula' is not a cover version. Manston and James were pseudonyms for Rossi and Young who adopted them, apparently, for reasons of copyright. The unusual title was arrived at by taking the names of two German fans, 'Gerd' and 'Ula', and pushing them together into a nonsense word. Lyrically the song is your standard 'man who has no luck with women' fare and bears no relation to the title or its namesakes. Musically it bounces along with an excellent Celtic flavoured instrumental in the middle where the tricky minor key melody is played in unison on electric and acoustic guitars, which is reprised for the fading coda section.

Dog Of Two Head

Personnel:
Francis Rossi: lead guitar, acoustic guitar, and vocals
Rick Parfitt: second guitar, acoustic guitar, piano, and vocals
Alan Lancaster: bass guitar, electric guitar
John Coghlan: drums, and percussion
Guest musicians:
Bob Young: harmonica
Bruce Foster: piano
Produced by John Schroeder
Engineer: Alan Florence
Recorded at Pye Records, London
Released on 5 November 1971
Highest chart position: Did not chart
Weeks on chart: Not applicable

Quo's second 'new era' album, and their last for Pye, gave fans just six new songs, and a re-recording of 'Gerdundula'. The label covered themselves with glory by misspelling Coghlan's surname on the sleeve (Coughlan), whilst Rossi was listed as Mike (one of his three middle names), and Rick Parfitt was, at the time, trading as Ritchie. By now, Pye had fundamentally lost interest in the band, and were happy to let them do pretty much what they wanted. This suited Quo down to the ground.

For their part, the band was building a solid reputation with relentless gigging all over the country. Slowly but surely, a dedicated group of fans grew and grew, eventually becoming known as the 'Quo Army'. By the middle of 1971, Quo were selling out gigs on the pub and club circuit and, whilst this work ethic didn't translate into album sales, it did ensure that they became a tight musical machine.

Another significant figure in Quo's history appeared in early 1971. The part-time managerial services of Pat Barlow were dispensed with, and Colin Johnson, who ran his own agency 'Exclusive Artists', became their full-time manager. Johnson made the necessary decision to get the band out of their contract with Pye, although a further album and single was still required. The band therefore issued a farewell '45' for the label, 'Tune To The Music' in June 1971. It failed to chart.

The songs for *Dog...*, as had been the case with *Ma Kelly*, were already up and running. The 'writing-on-the-road/trialling-at-gigs' approach delivered the goods again. Apart from the unremarkable 'Na Na Na', *Dog...* showed the band's commitment to authentic blues rock, as exemplified by the inside of the album's gatefold cover. There is an image of the band in energetic form live on stage, together with four individual black and white portrait photos. Lancaster is playing cards, Parfitt is concentrating on his guitar, Rossi looks purposefully into the middle distance, whilst Coghlan is caught in a 'mouth open whilst drumming' moment. No one is remotely close to smiling; these are pictures of the young men as serious musicians. The album's title is credited to Paul Lodge, one of the band's crew, who christened their equipment van 'Dog Of Two Head'. The front cover is a garish image of a black and white two-headed bulldog imposed over a picture of Windsor Castle, and some other typically English views, all mounted on a bright red background. The illustration was by Mick Wells, based upon a design by the band. Four small versions of the individual photos of Parfitt, Rossi, Lancaster, and Coghlan decorate the corners, and the songs' lyrics were included. This was clearly part of the grown-up business of making a full-on rock album.

Dog... saw the band cut all ties with their previous pop and psychedelic inclinations and contained, in the main, nothing but hard-nosed, powerful music. Here they are a creative, potent force, making their name in a disciplined, hardworking fashion. For once *Dog...* did get the band some proper promotional attention. David 'Kid' Jensen presented a progressive music show on Radio Luxemburg at the time:

> I thought it was a great rock album. I'd loved 'Down The Dustpipe', of course, but unbelievably they were still put in that whole Marmalade/Casuals bag, despite what they were doing live. I just went ahead and played the album and ignored what was meant to be fashionable. They were a great, go-ahead, steaming rock band.

Dog... is loud and brash, confident and ambitious. It is further confirmation of the band's direction, with an overall harder and heavier sound than *Ma Kelly's...* . Whilst John Schroeder was listed as producer his involvement was much less than had been the case with previous albums. Quo were finding their musical feet in the studio, and learning to self-produce their material. The results are dramatic, and laid the ground for the next five albums. There are no cover versions, and the recurring 'Na Na Na' is the only truly acoustic number.

Whilst *Ma Kelly...* hadn't served up any classics, *Dog...* showed the growing influence of the song-writing partnership of Rossi and Young, giving fans two early favourites in 'Mean Girl' and 'Railroad'. Lancaster's heavyweight contributions should not be overlooked either; the bassist's songs provided a weighty counterbalance to the album's occasionally lighter moments, whilst Parfitt is curiously absent from the song writing credits.

The departure of Roy Lynes is barely noticed and, when a song required a keyboard, a session player would be drafted in for the role. This was the *modus operandi* until 1977, when Andy Bown would become a permanent band member, although he didn't enjoy official membership accreditation until 1982.

Across Quo's first two 'serious rock' albums and their non-album singles of the period, a total of 20 tracks, only three ('Spinning Wheel Blues', 'Lazy Poker Blues', and 'Down The Dustpipe') stay in the lane of straight twelve-bar. Although 'Mean Girl' and 'Railroad' have twelve-bar elements, 75% of the band's last two releases for Pye are straight hard rock. Whilst some of the songs have a twelve-bar shuffle *feel*, other tracks (including '(April), Spring, Summer, and Wednesdays' and 'Gerdundula') have no such reference points, and stand alone as individual creations with strong melodic and rhythmic spines.

'Umleitung' (Lancaster/Lynes) Duration: 7.10 Chord Count: 4

Recalling the stop/start elements of '(April), Spring, Summer, and Wednesdays' and 'Is It Really Me?', the brief introduction soon settles into a shuffle groove over a steady 4/4 rhythm, with a constant minor pentatonic riff revolving away in the background. Against this, temporary keyboard player Bruce Foster hammers out relentlessly repetitive C7 chords. This sets up a slight but effective harmonic tension in the accompaniment.

'Umleitung' (the German for 'diversion') may refer to a romantic interlude as the refrain implies; 'Woman can I come? Woman, can I come to you? 'Cos I need your love, yes I need your love'. Equally, the relentless rhythmic backing and drone-style texture provides a hypnotic audio distraction. Whatever the true explanation, the title does not feature in the lyrics. After two verses, the track stretches its musical legs.

There is a lengthy guitar solo over a relentless, catatonic, C minor backing from 1.23 to 4.52, with Foster bashing the ivories with gusto behind Rossi's spiky, melodic phrases. The opening verses are repeated, then Rossi and Parfitt briefly play the shuffle chords in unison (6.07-6.16) before the singer is off up the fretboard again, whilst the heavy twelve-bar shuffle rhythm alternates between C and F major. A reprise of the introduction rolls into repeated triplets, three power chords, and a tight ending for this overly long and yet, paradoxically, trance-like, engaging number.

'Umleitung' is a brave opening assault, long on solos and simplistic by design, it highlights the band's wish to be taken seriously. *Dog...*', while possessing a more cohesively heavy rock sound, still had the capacity to surprise…

'Na Na Na' (Rossi/Young) Duration: 0.51 Chord Count: 8

The solo acoustic guitar introduction of triplet arpeggios based in the key of D minor chord is reminiscent of Tony Iommi's similar instrumental miniatures on the early Black Sabbath albums.

The song itself is in D major, in 2/4 time with a jaunty country feel. Some bouncy piano joins Parfitt's strumming and Rossi's vocals ('Writing songs that I think sound so strange, writing words that I feel I should change, It's all right if they sound just like other songs, my guitar strums along just the same, if the song's underlined with my name') fade just before the first chorus.

'Something Going On In My Head' (Lancaster) Duration: 4.42 Chord Count: 8

The album finally moves up a gear with this fine slice of up-tempo boogie action. A single swinging grind of a guitar riff is joined by a second six string, and bass and drums kick in to a Lancaster song where Rossi again takes the lead vocal. The chorus, 'Something's going on in my head ... and I'm not quite sure what you said', is catchy with effective harmony vocals, and the music comes to a sudden stop at the end of the first chorus.

The riff starts again with added impetus and power into a second verse and chorus, which is followed by a single 2/4 rest bar before moving into a new section (1.36-1.50) with some persuasive, choral style backing vocals. Underpinning this are some tight triplet rhythms and then a lengthy Rossi solo then takes hold, the majority of which (2.04-3.42) occurs over a single chord backing. This is where interest starts to wane, and the final verse and chorus are very welcome when they arrive. The song fades with a reprise of the 'choral' section.

'Something Going On In My Head' is an overlooked gem in the early years of Quo, showing a winning combination of melody and power, which they would later harness to even greater effect. The song is something of a 'deep cut' in the Quo archive, which is a shame as its energy, craft, and creativity suggests it deserved more audience credit than it ever received. As it stands, it's an excellent track, and more than holds its own on the album.

'Mean Girl' (Rossi/Young) Duration: 3.52 Chord Count: 10

A quintessential Quo song, 'Mean Girl' hits the ground running and doesn't let up. There's a ferocious energy to the track which starts with some brutal sustained power chords before dropping into a higher-than-usual pitched rhythm guitar shuffle. Lyrically it's, shall we say, 'of its time' and is an early example of the wordplay which Bob Young was fond of. What carries the song is the memorable and insistent chorus, where a second voice, probably Parfitt, joins Rossi in unison.

The instrumental section (1.13-1.53) has Rossi's fingers dancing all over his fretboard, whilst the rest of the band are as rhythmically tight as the grip of the proverbial tyre fitter's hand. At 2.15, there is a fabulous display of quick, chord changes which are inserted into the repeat of the opening verse. Another instrumental interlude is full of fire and attitude, until 3.23 when the power gradually subsides for a slower coda section. Foster throws in some fine piano flourishes to conclude the song, which fades on a sustained seventh chord.

'Na Na Na' (Rossi/Young) Duration: 1.10 Chord Count: 8

It's back. This time we get to the end of the first chorus, which has some pleasing harmony vocals, before the fade.

'Gerdundula' (Manston/James) Duration: 3.49 Chord Count: 5

Fading in with guitar feedback giving a good impression of sustained Indian style drones, this is a re-recording of the song from the *Ma Kelly...* period. Here the instrumentation is all-electric with some energetic handclaps in place of Coghlan's bongos, and Rossi's solos are joined by a tambourine in the mix. Altogether this gives the song a stronger, rockier, and slightly faster feel. The electrified remake lasts longer than the more acoustic original, and comes to a definitive end rather than a fade. This involves a reprise of the instrumental section with a neat use of reducing dynamics in the coda before building into a powerful last phrase.

This isn't the last time 'Gerdundula' would be recorded. Another version of it appeared on the 'Roll Over Lay Down' EP in May 1975. The song has also been a staple number in the band's live set at various stages during their career, and is a perfect example of a very different side to Quo for their numerous critics. It's melodic, well arranged, memorable, and not as easy to play as your ears may think. But, you know, 'all their songs sound the same to me'. Well, you haven't listened to all their songs then, have you...?

'Railroad' (Rossi/Young) Duration: 5.27 Chord Count: 10

Like 'Mean Girl', 'Railroad' is a song more closely aligned to a twelve-bar format, but both tracks are anything but straightforward. 'Railroad', especially, highlights the band's capacity for creative compositions with impressive dynamic and textural control; in effect, innovation within excellent rocking music.

'Railroad' is really three separate, completely different compositions joined together to make one big one. The first segment is a rollicking, up-tempo shuffle with a revolving minor pentatonic blues riff filling out the sound. Starting with a harmonised chorus, the riff disappears for Rossi's solitary verse under some solid shuffle grooving. A repeat of the chorus leads into a short section of power chords which ushers in the second instalment.

Part two (1.47-2.20) is a short instrumental duet for plucked acoustic guitar and mournful harmonica. This calm atmosphere is shattered by the third song, which is a brutally heavy, slow blues. The highlight of this section is Young and his skilful ability to make the harmonica *sound* so anguished, and is perfectly suited to the heavyweight rhythmic backing.

Parfitt takes over the vocals for a typical blues lyric, 'Her face was always smiling, yeah she was always laughing at me...'. At 3.50, Rossi contributes appropriately pained phrases for his solo, before being joined by Young for the final crushing pass through the chord sequence, and a heavily strummed finish.

'Someone's Learning' (Lancaster) Duration: 7.07 Chord Count: 5

Epic is the best word for the album's second longest and most persuasive track. Multi-faceted and making full use of dynamic light and shade, 'Someone's Learning' prefigures lengthy songs like '4500 Times' and 'Slow Train' in the degree of skill in its composition and arrangement.

Opening with some gently strummed chords, and subtle high register bass as a counterpoint, a simply mahoosive riff then bulldozes its way to the front with

Rossi's vocals too far back in the mix. The chorus is powerful and melodic, with a rising bass line neatly complementing the powerful rhythm section. There is a clever arrangement of instruments going on here. Parfitt's chords, Lancaster's harmonised bass and Rossi's interweaving melody under the chorus lyrics form an impressive triptych of sound.

At 1.25, the power comes down again for a reprise of the opening; then the riff crashes in again for a second verse and chorus. Quo are rarely celebrated for their lyrics, but here Lancaster provides some thought-provoking lines; 'In the night three children died, now all were under five, that's alright, God's on our side, now, our religion's right', reflecting the conflict known as 'The Troubles' which was taking place in Northern Ireland at the time.

A brief drum break at 2.47 leads into the instrumental section, where Rossi and Parfitt play a melody in octaves before a wild solo section breaks out (3.21) over a single chord accompaniment. At 4.25, the volume quietens, but it's a temporary lull as Rossi introduces a repetitive short phrase which Parfitt then harmonises, the rhythm section volume suddenly increasing. Drums and bass stop, leaving the harmonised guitars playing their joint, siren style melody continuously until 5.10. It's impressive stuff and shows that genuine creativity will always win out over loose, meandering improvisation. Here the music is tightly controlled, well thought out, and played with a degree of technical accuracy which critics prefer to overlook.

There's a return to the introduction with another powerful verse and chorus before a final play-through of the introduction. This builds in volume and distortion before a pounding, repeated A major chord brings this impressive composition to a staccato finish.

'Na Na Na' (Rossi/Young) Duration: 2.23 Chord Count: 8

Finally presented in all its glory, 'Na Na Na' really hasn't been worth the wait. It's a pleasing enough ode to the pleasure of writing songs and performing live, even if your audience isn't particularly persuaded by your talent.

The song passes a couple of minutes without incident, but a better number, like 'Tune To The Music', would have been more appropriate. The backing vocals are credited to 'Grass' who were a support group for Quo during this period.

Non-Album Tracks
'Tune To The Music' (Rossi/Young) Duration: 3.06 Chord Count: 6

Similar in energy level to 'Mean Girl' but with a poppier feel, 'Tune To The Music' is a brisk shuffle with some fast-paced melodic lead inserts. Rossi's vocals are at the front of the mix, and the whole song powers along enthusiastically following a conventional verse/chorus/repeat structure. There's some busy soloing in the closing seconds before the quick fade.

'Good Thinking' (Status Quo) Duration: 3.40 Chord Count: 3

This was the B-side to 'Tune To The Music'. It's a throwaway shuffle blues instrumental which sounds like a recorded jam or rehearsal. Rossi solos throughout and your life is not diminished in any way if you've not heard this.

Piledriver

Personnel:
Francis Rossi: lead guitar, 12 string and acoustic guitars, vocals
Rick Parfitt: second guitar, acoustic guitar, piano, organ, vocals
Alan Lancaster: bass guitar, 12 string acoustic guitar, vocals
John Coghlan: drums, and percussion
Guest musicians:
Bob Young: harmonica
Jimmy Horrowitz: piano
Produced by Status Quo
Engineered by Damon Lyon-Shaw
Recorded at IBC Studios, London
Released on 20 January 1973
Highest chart position: 5
Weeks on chart: 38

Colin Johnson could see that Quo were destined for bigger and better things. He extricated the band from their contract with Pye, signed them to Gaff Management, and engineered a transfer to Vertigo, a subsidiary of the Phonogram label.

Established in 1969, Vertigo was a home for the emerging progressive rock scene; bands that were focused on album releases rather than single chart success. They were a 'Rock-As-Art' label, and Quo joined a roster that included Black Sabbath, Uriah Heep, and The Sensational Alex Harvey Band, amongst others. Vertigo and Quo was an ideal fit, and reinforced their determination to be treated as an albums band by an album orientated label.

Following the release of *Dog...* the band continued their relentless touring schedule. In September 1972, they began recording new songs at IBC Studios in Portland Place, London, without the services of John Schroeder. Johnson suggested the band self produce the first release for their new label. It was an inspired idea. Schroeder had been more of an overseer than an actual producer for *Ma Kelly...* and *Dog...* Despite their relative lack of recording experience, Quo knew what they wanted to achieve: the 'live-in-the-studio' sound. In effect, this meant setting the equipment up as they would for a gig, and pressing 'record'. In the sleeve notes to the 2006 CD reissue of *Piledriver*. Rossi said

> We were out on our own, and we knew it. In fact we'd been on our own for years, only this time it was us, not a record company, not a producer, that was going to make the decisions. We wanted to get across on record what we meant on stage, for our own sakes and for the fans.

Seven years after their first record contract, and five years on from 'Pictures Of Matchstick Men', Quo finally returned to the singles chart. 'Paper Plane' was released on 10 November 1972, backed with 'Softer Ride', a song which would appear on the subsequent album *Hello!* Record company support took the form of full-page adverts in the music press, and a special 'A' label promotional single for radio stations ensured that the track reached number eight in the charts. Vocal support from John Peel and 'Kid' Jensen, influential disc jockeys of the time, did nothing to harm its progress. At the time Rossi acknowledged the new success to a reporter on *Disc* magazine:

It's great to be back in the chart again because the success this time is built on something concrete which we've established since the end of '69. We didn't go out and consciously write the song as a single, it was just the right length and had plenty of balls.

'Paper Plane' spent eleven weeks in the chart and started a run of 34 consecutive hits for the band. Pye Records was smarting at their lost opportunity, and a subsequent court injunction prevented the release of *Piledriver*. Eventually, the new album entered the UK charts at the end of January 1973 at number 5. Rossi saw its success as a direct correlation to the years of hard work the band had put in:

'Before the single and the album we'd built up a large following and were pulling good crowds, but the single and LP have really opened up everything for the band'.

Quoted in *The Status Quo Autobiography – XS All Areas* Rossi said of the solitary single

Despite our newfound success, we desperately wanted to be taken seriously as an album-orientated band. In the early Seventies, a real album-orientated band only released one single per album. Therefore, that's what we did too, and no immediate follow up to 'Paper Plane' was scheduled.

That didn't stop Pye from trying to capitalise on Quo's newfound success by releasing a 'follow-up' single to 'Paper Plane' on 22 January 1973. 'Mean Girl', backed with 'Everything' reached number 20 as part of an eleven-week run. In July 1973, Pye had another go when 'Gerdundula' backed with 'Lakky Lady' emerged, but this failed to chart.

This wasn't the end of Pye's exploitation of the empty stable now the thoroughbred had found its legs and bolted. A compilation album *The Best Of Status Quo* appeared in 1973 and concentrated, wisely, on material from *Ma Kelly...* and *Dog....* It did well, reaching 32 in the charts. June 1973 saw the release of a compilation of the pre-'Frantic Four' with its focus on *Picturesque Matchstickable Messages...* and *Spare Parts*. This appeared on Pye's subsidiary label, 'Golden Hour', and completely misrepresented the music contained therein. The sleeve depicted Rossi, Parfitt, and Lancaster in full heads down, hair flowing rock mode, a pose Parfitt would later refer to as 'the attack stance', which bore no relationship to the music on the record.

The cover for *Piledriver* was also a markedly superior idea. The new album showed the world exactly what Quo were about. Parfitt, Rossi, and Lancaster are shown in close formation, heads down no-nonsense boogie mode. Coghlan is nowhere to be seen, but it's very likely he's behind all the hair somewhere. The album title was suggested by Colin Johnson, believing that the wrestling term would be an appropriate summary of what the audience could expect for their money. Like *Dog...*, *Piledriver* featured a gatefold sleeve, with the lyrics included amidst pictures of the band in five sweaty, live-action scenes.

On the back of the cover was a cartoon image of a gorilla carrying a bomb with the word 'Piledriver', emblazoned in capitals. It was this 'monkey and missile' image which would begin the fashion of putting a small black and white image of preceding album covers on the rear sleeve of any new release, adding the words 'From The Makers Of....' In effect, this was the band disowning the three albums they had released prior to *Dog...*, which does *Ma Kelly...* a disservice.

Whilst *Piledriver* is the third of Quo's trio of 'all serious' albums, it differs significantly from *Ma Kelly...* and *Dog...* in its sound. This is due to the way the songs were now being recorded. John Schroeder had followed the time-honoured method; direct injection of each instrument's tones into the recording desk to achieve as much separation in the individual sounds as possible, before then mixing the constituent parts back together. The development of new, louder, and better sounding guitar amplifiers by the likes of Marshall, Orange, and Vox meant that bands wanted the bigger, warmer sound such equipment supplied to be captured on tape. For Quo, this meant recording themselves at stage volumes. It was another inspired decision. *Ma Kelly's...* and *Dog...*, whilst good, had a distinct clarity between the instruments. *Piledriver* turned this on its head. At times it's brutal, almost out of control, and immensely liberating. Again the band avoids the temptation for 'look at me' showmanship, opting instead for a breathtaking combined assault of two electric guitars, a bass, and a drum kit, (with occasional keyboards in support,) acting as a single, overwhelming force.

Piledriver proved to be the breakthrough album which Quo richly deserved. And yet, despite its 'take-no-prisoners' attitude, the record is too ballad-heavy. Three of the songs are softer numbers. Whilst it's good to show you're not a one-trick pony, the overall balance is skewed, especially in the sequencing of the tracks. After the *blitzkrieg* of 'Don't Waste My Time', and 'Oh Baby', the next ten minutes is taken up with the understated 'A Year', and the slow blues of 'Unspoken Words'. Fortunately, full power is restored with 'Big Fat Mama', and the rest of the album is massively satisfying. I can still recall my relative disappointment on first hearing this LP, that half of the former 'side one' was so introspective and 'un-Quo-like'. Time has not altered my opinion. The success of *Piledriver* meant that the band's contract with Vertigo was extended and improved. The label knew they were onto something special. They were right.

'Don't Waste My Time' (Rossi/Young) Duration: 4.20 Chord Count: 9

Piledriver is *loud!* Rossi's siren-sounding introduction opens proceedings, and then the rhythm section just, ahem, pile in and go for it. 'Don't Waste My Time' is a riot of brazen electric guitars, heavy bass, and relentless drums. Rossi's vocal takes a one-sided relationship and turns it on its head; here it is the female who is just out for a good time, whilst the male wants something more meaningful. Parfitt joins in on the refrain, 'You spend my money, c'mon honey don't waste my time', and Rossi's solo after the second refrain is bitingly melodic.

The third verse is a repeat of the first, and another solo follows before a break at 3.23, where we hear Parfitt's rhythm guitar alone in all its amplified glory. Shouts of approval can just about be heard in the background before Lancaster and Coghlan batter down the doors and the aural assault continues. Rossi provides another trebly, ear-bleeding solo to the bluesy close.

'O Baby' (Rossi/Parfitt) Duration: 4.38 Chord Count: 5

Starting with a slow fade in of electric guitars quietly playing a rising melody and chord progression, the volume gradually increases. Lancaster and Coghlan then bulldoze their way into the song with a heavy 'four to the floor' riff, which breaks into the double time verse at 0.58.

Rossi and Parfitt sing the vocal melody in unison before the song shifts into a solo at 1.50, which combines elements of country and rockabilly against the relentless rhythm. At 2.17, a new dual guitar melody takes centre stage, with some tight playing leading back into a reprise of the heavy opening riff. The first two verses are repeated, and the song rocks off into the distance with the secondary instrumental riff bending the putty in the windows.

'O Baby' is an overlooked powerhouse of a track which the band would, surprisingly, resuscitate for the 'Frantic Four' reunion tours of 2013 and 2014.

'A Year' (Frost/Lancaster) Duration: 5.45 Chord Count: 9

A ballad to take the mood down and show the range of your musicianship and song writing you say? Oh, go on then…

'A Year' is an abrupt 180-degree change of mood. It has strong echoes of 'While My Guitar Gently Weeps' by The Beatles, both in its repeated descending chord progression, and the modulation to the parallel key of A major for the mid-section. It is musically mournful and lyrically mourning. Writing about the death of a loved one is an unusual subject for a rock band, and the intense subject matter is handled tastefully. Rossi's vocals are suitably plaintive, and his guitar embellishments add much to the texture. There is rise and fall in the dynamics and careful arrangement in the music to prevent aural boredom from setting in.

At 1.49, the new major key section begins, 'How could I ever start to tell you, the end is almost here, the song of love is ringing in my ears, playing loud, playing clear, the song will never change, the memory will always be so near'. Vocal harmonies change the emphasis of this section of the music. A sustained organ adds much to the positive feel, with Lancaster providing melodic bass lines before the music relaxes back into its initial mood.

The opening verse, 'Standing by the wayside, begging for a ride, I been waiting so long, a year has gone' is accompanied by some arpeggios which may have been 'inspired' by Led Zeppelin's 'Stairway To Heaven'. This leads into Rossi's lengthy, emotive solo, which runs from 3.11 to the song's end. The tension builds throughout, Lancaster being especially prominent compared to Coghlan's busy, but way-back-in-the-mix, drumming.

The solo concludes at 4.41, leading to some more instrumental music with heightened dynamics before finally coming to rest on an A minor chord. This is, unfortunately, unbalanced by the vibration of the guitar's low E string against the rest of the notes. 'A Year' is a beautiful, if overly long song, but pile-driving it certainly isn't.

'Unspoken Words' (Rossi/Young) Duration: 5.07 Chord Count: 8

'Unspoken Words' is a more traditional, slow blues track, enhanced by some evocative organ and Rossi's highly charged solo playing. But the passion and power evinced on the first two tracks have by now been completely dissipated. Saying that, there's nothing wrong with the song at all; Parfitt is in fine voice and, as a demonstration of the varied textures the band was capable of creating, it's a highly effective piece of music.

Back in 1972, there was an approximate maximum of 40 minutes in which to set out your vinyl stall. Whilst 'Unspoken Words' is miles ahead of some of the music the band would produce post *Blue For You*, another rocker would have been *much* more welcome as a 'side closer'. Rossi's lead work is the high point of this track; his guitar tone is exceptional, his phrasing and melodic lines are packed with intense emotion, and he isn't scared of allowing musical space in his playing to enhance the effectiveness of the sound.

'Big Fat Mama' (Parfitt/Rossi) Duration: 5.53 Chord Count: 10

Aha, Status Quo the rock band, welcome back, how we've missed you! A multi-faceted brute of a track, 'Big Fat Mama' is a six-sectioned song which grabs you by the ears and, with only a brief mid-song interlude, doesn't let go until nearly six minutes later. Lancaster commented on the song's gestation in a radio interview in November 1975:

> It took us months to do that track, sitting in rehearsals, George IV pub in Brixton, next to the prison. Rick comes up with this song, wasn't a song really,

just bits of arrangement and we spent rehearsals and rehearsals trying to do something with it, but it just wouldn't come together. A few months later, Francis did something with it and I worked on it...

Certainly 'Big Fat Mama' was the band's most ambitious work to date. The introduction (0.00 – 0.17) is a tight-knit display of unison electric guitars. Lancaster's bass is introduced, and the music separates into octaves as Coghlan's aggressive drumming joins the fray. And then we're into the first song of what is, in reality, a two-part epic. The riff is spectacular; fast, powerful and committed. Parfitt takes the vocals in both parts, the first being a relentless plea to an unspecified woman over some furious chordal drive. This culminates in some impressive unison playing around the refrain, 'I am yours, tonight, you be mine, tonight' before coming to an abrupt halt. The reprieve is only temporary, however as the guitars blast in again, and it's off into a second verse and refrain we go.

The first of two distinct instrumental sections is at 2.28. This is another display of solid unison playing of an intricate melody, first *pianissimo* and then reverting to full thunder. At 2.53, there is a respite with an atmospheric, melodic guitar line. Plenty of reverb has been added to enhance the mood over the tense-sounding chord progression.

At 3.20, the second song takes flight as a supremely heavy rhythm grabs hold, and the object of Parfitt's affection is revealed. You don't enjoy 'Big Fat Mama' for its poetic lyrics, the words don't matter at all. The underlying music is just magnificent, loud, powerful, and compelling. The final section is Rossi's solo at 4.19, which drives along to the heavy power chord conclusion that finally closes with a brief echo effect.

'Big Fat Mama', the second-longest track on *Piledriver*, and its lengthiest original composition, is an overwhelming display of musical power with elements of progressive rock mixed in with blues rock to maximum effect.

'Paper Plane' (Rossi/Young) Duration: 2.57 Chord Count: 3

A spectacular three-chord blitz on the senses, 'Paper Plane' is the perfect blend of power, melody, and commercial catchiness which showcases Quo at one of their several bests. Notwithstanding the psychedelic/drug stimulated nature of some of Young's words ('Riding on a big white butterfly, I turned my back away towards the sky'), Rossi's characteristically reedy vocals ride over the intense rhythmic drive with sonic space only appearing for the short refrain, 'We all make mistakes forgive me'.

The double stop solo is fast, furious and melodic, with descending octave lines at 1.55. Again this is an example of Rossi not overplaying. It's a perfect opportunity amongst all the energy and *élan* of the song to let fly, but he remains controlled, and yet still supremely effective. The third verse has a reference to a 'three grand Deutsche car', a Mercedes, which was the band's new purchase, getting a special mention. The song fades quickly on a reprise of the rapid instrumental section.

Utterly fantastic five decades on 'Paper Plane' is the perfect calling card for the classic rock band which Quo would rightly claim as their success in the Seventies showed.

'All The Reasons' (Lancaster/Parfitt) Duration: 3.38 Chord Count: 4

'All The Reasons' is the best of the album's three ballads. Tightly structured, well arranged, with layers of instrumentation and concise delivery, it shows Quo at their laid back, melodic best.

Opening with a three-part harmonised guitar sequence which has an anthemic feel to it, with some nice bass counterpoint and suitable percussive touches from Coghlan, the song moves into some pretty arpeggiated chords, as Parfitt's gentle voice handles the lyrics with care; 'When I find myself in trouble and I need someone to lean on, I only have to call and you're right there by my side...'. Yes, you're right, it's a long way from Shakespeare, but it sounds sincere.

At 1.30, Rossi has a simple high register tune as a solo, with Coghlan adding subtle drums. For the second verse, there are some melodic lower bass lines, which continue the lyrical mood. The lead guitar line is repeated at 2.27 with Coghlan going into double time as the music moves into a reprise of the introductory section. Parfitt's understated vocals weave in and out as this impressive song fades away.

'Roadhouse Blues' (Densmore/Krieger/Manzarek/Morrison) Duration: 7.25 Chord Count: 8

To misquote Michael Caine; Quo's 'Roadhouse Blues' blows the bloody Doors away. Starting with a count in and some brief piano chords, the song gets an absolutely monstrous makeover in this dynamically varied cover version. Both Young's harmonica and Horrowitz's keyboard make welcome and effective contributions, and Lancaster's gruff vocal tone works well over the relentless rhythm.

Rossi has an excellent solo (1.40 – 3.14) which would set the template for the extended live versions. This studio take doesn't extend to include his rendition of 'The Mexican Hat Dance', which would feature regularly on stage. The volume drops down three and a half minutes in with a repeat of the first verse as the vocals go into three-part harmony before the volume rises again for 'Let it roll...all night long' section. It's back to (relative) subtlety for the next verse and Young's harmonica solo (5.20 – 6.00).

Lancaster takes it easy with the verse, 'I should've made you... give up your vows', before the power returns for the remainder of the verse. There is a full-throated final chorus, a rising chromatic chord sequence, topped off with a brief flourish from Rossi, and the song ends with what sounds like a 'God, that was fun' relaxed bass and drum punch as the guitars fade.

Quo were never averse to covering other artists' songs and frequently had chart success with them, but 'Roadhouse Blues' is the definitive example of taking something that wasn't at all bad to begin with, and transforming it into a number which is markedly superior to the original.

Hello!

Personnel:
Francis Rossi: lead and various guitars, vocals
Richard Parfitt: second and various guitars, vocals
Alan Lancaster: bass guitar, vocals
John Coghlan: drums, and various percussion
Guest musicians:
Andy Bown: piano on 'Blue Eyed Lady'
John Mealing: piano on 'Forty Five Hundred Times'
Steve Farr: alto saxophone
Stewart Blandamer: tenor saxophone
Produced by Status Quo
Robert Young: coordinator
Damon Lyon-Shaw: first engineer
Richard Mainwaring: second engineer
Recorded at IBC Studios, London
Released on 6 October 1973
Highest chart position: 1
Weeks on chart: 28

Quo's next album went straight into the charts at number one. Just take a
moment to let that fact sink in. The successes of *Piledriver*, and the 45 'Paper
Plane', together with the band's incredibly hard gigging schedule paid off in
spades. However, the unspoken words on everybody's mind were 'hit single'.
Rossi, in particular, was worried that 'Paper Plane' might be to the new Quo
what 'Pictures Of Matchstick Men' had been to the old, in effect, a one-hit
wonder. In *I Talk Too Much*, he admitted:

> No one was pushing the point, but I knew in my bones that the thing that
> would really keep the show on the road was another hit single ... I wouldn't
> have said it out loud at the time, but that is how I was feeling as we got ready
> to make *(Hello!)*

Rossi need not have been worried. The next hit began life as a country-style
ditty written by Rossi and Bob Young three years previously on a joint family
holiday in Cornwall. Once the song was given to the rest of the band, it became
transformed into an out-and-out classic rocker. 'Caroline', the only single to be
released from *Hello!*, appeared in August 1973, hitting number five in the charts.
   The cover of the new album was a stark contrast to what fans were used
to seeing. Instead of a colourful gatefold, *Hello!* was issued in a matt black
single sleeve. Tilting the cover into the light revealed a glossy silhouette of
the four men standing together. Left to right, Parfitt and Rossi have their right
arms raised aloft, Coghlan has his sticks in the air, and Lancaster is raising his
bass in his right hand. Beneath the image, the album title was printed in grey

in a handwriting style font. *Hello!* was also notable for the introduction of the slanted and shaded design of the band's name. This would become their official logo, appearing on nearly all subsequent releases, merchandise, concert programmes, *et al.*

The inner sleeve contained the lyrics printed white on black, and a large poster was included as part of the package; Coghlan, Parfitt, and Rossi stand moodily behind Lancaster, who poses on the floor. There wasn't a hint of the bright colours of *Piledriver* anywhere to be seen. This was, again, Quo wanting to be both seen and heard as serious rock musicians.

Hello!, the title being another Colin Johnson suggestion, is also significant for the first appearance of keyboard player Andy Bown, formerly of The Herd. The innovative inclusion of alto and tenor saxophones is almost inaudible in the mix, and Bob Young must have lost his harmonica as his contribution is listed merely as 'co-ordinator', whatever that means. For the new album, Quo used the same recording approach as *Piledriver*; the 'live volume in the studio' sound. There was no let-up either in the relentless touring schedule, which meant that new compositions were again premiered to the audience, possibly refined, and finally honed into definitive beasts for the studio.

Hello! is a mighty piece of work offering up three classics in 'Caroline', 'Roll Over Lay Down', and the epic 'Forty Five Hundred Times'. The less well-known songs, however, maintain the high quality levels. 'A Reason For Living' is an uplifting stomper, and 'Blue Eyed Lady' shows the band hadn't lost their technical chops in another heads down onslaught. There is the first nod towards country rock with 'Claudie', plenty of light and shade in the powerful 'Softer Ride', and a single, excellent ballad in 'And It's Better Now'.

It's this relative softening and occasional lightening of mood which marks the beginning of the next significant shift in Quo's history. This is the gradual move away from the tone established with *Dog...* and *Piledriver*, with the first examples of pop rock and country influences entering the bands hard-rocking mainstream. *Hello!* is a transition album from the outright power of most of *Piledriver* to a more varied sonic palette. The emphasis on lighter styles of writing would increase and meant the band would be increasingly successful from a commercial standpoint. Until 1977 this balance was kept under strict control and produced most of their best material. After that, the needle swung too far in the other direction for many long-term fans.

'Roll Over Lay Down' (Rossi/Young/Lancaster/Parfitt/Coghlan) Duration: 5.40 Chord Count: 7

One of the few Quo songs to have an official five-way writing credit is actually another Rossi/Young composition. Colin Johnson had talked the pair into this as the royalties from song writing were beginning to cause some disquiet within the band.

Internal politics aside, 'Roll Over Lay Down' is fantastic. Bouncing along with a heavy shuffle rhythm, Rossi's shrill Telecaster plays the verse melody and a refrain over the chorus chord sequence as an introduction. Despite the obvious innuendo of the lyrics, Rossi, the vocalist, has always maintained that the song actually concerns the fact that his then wife would sleep on 'his' side of the bed, and in trying to move her the phrase 'Roll over, lay down and let me in' came about. Okay, if you say so.

The verses have effective power chords rising in-between the lyric lines, and the chorus is infectiously catchy with effective harmony vocals. Following the second chorus, there is a one bar rest before the instrumental, which is in two parts. The first has Rossi developing bluesy phrases over the solid rhythmic backing. This breaks into louder life at 2.12, with the solo becoming busier whilst still maintaining a highly melodic core. At 2.42, the rhythm section reverts to playing sustained power chords before the first half of the instrumental appears to come to a close at 3.05.

The second half begins with a quiet, understated lead guitar melody over Parfitt's arpeggios and root notes from Lancaster. The key has changed from D minor, which has dominated the music up to this point, to D major. Gradually, the power begins to build with Coghlan playing rapid triplet rolls under the steady 4/4 rhythm. The volume gradually returns to maximum, and Rossi reprises the second verse as the third and final one. There is another chorus before the concluding solo over the verse chord sequence, which builds to a climax, with chords rising before the song ends with a squeal of controlled feedback.

What makes 'Roll Over Lay Down' so special is the band's use of dynamics, a technique that is often overlooked with Quo songs. Whilst composing in what can be an uncomplicated genre may seem simple, it's what you do to the music which transforms it. Here, especially, Quo completely understand and implement the power of volume changes necessary to make a track completely compelling.

'Claudie' (Rossi/Young) Duration: 4.02 Chord Count: 5
This is a happily jaunty rock-meets-country tune that prefigures 'Fine, Fine, Fine' from the band's next album. 'Claudie' is in D major, which provides a cheery backdrop to the morose 'end of relationship' lyric; the narrator looks back to a time when he and Claudie shared a home, which he has now moved out of.

Starting with a rising major scale, the song quickly kicks into a medium tempo. The verse's vocal melody is strong and again, the chorus is catchy. There are vague undertones of early Beatles in the use of the G minor chord under the word 'place' in the line, 'With Claudie is the *place* I want to be'.

It sounds like Rossi is having a ball in the solo section. His country-rock phrases work well against the thundering rhythm section, which leads back into a repeat of the introduction before the final verse and chorus. This features harmony vocals adding atmosphere to the lines 'When I left did you think of me crying, did you care that I felt I was dying', which occurs again in the final line, 'I'm a fool, little Claudie just for you' before the song powers into the final chorus.

It is this strange juxtaposition of positive-sounding accompaniment to a mournful lyric of heartbreak which places the listener's ears in an odd place. We're not sure whether to empathise with the words or simply enjoy the music. There is no dynamic change or tempo alteration in the song; it starts as it means to go on and fades quickly after the final chorus.

'A Reason For Living' (Rossi/Parfitt) Duration: Chord Count: 6

One of Quo's few forays into religion and, unlike many rock bands who were critical of the subject, the lyrics are, by the second verse, surprisingly positive and reassuring, 'So I knelt down by my bedside, and I started to say a prayer, it was when I asked for nothing I could feel that there was somebody there'.

Musically 'A Reason For Living' is on the simplistic side, although the arrangement of the instruments is well executed. The song bounces along happily with a solid guitar rhythm, and the rest of the band crash in for the second verse with some effective piano and slide guitar fills. This leads into another melodic solo from Rossi, the second part with its feet planted firmly back in 'Claudie's country turf. The third verse benefits from a full-frontal instrumental mix and harmony vocals, and there is a brief reprise of the first section of the solo before the music slows dramatically at 3.18 into a slow blues. This is similar to the third part of the 'Railroad' track before the number comes to a standard ending for the genre.

What spoils the song, and darkens the tone of the entire album, is the degree of reverb applied to the production. It's too much in places, and leaves the band sounding mushy and boomy, rather than punchy and direct.

'Blue Eyed Lady' (Lancaster/Parfitt) Duration: 3.49 Chord Count: 7

'Blue Eyed Lady' has three separate introductions, all flowing into one another for the song's first 52 seconds. The first is a complex, rising staccato melody which wouldn't disgrace an early Yes album. The second part has a heavy country feel with staccato power chords in the rhythm section, which turns on the power before a sustained C major chord. Rossi alternates between minor and major third intervals as the volume grows. The final section has a descending run alternating between an underlying C major and G major, which leads into a pulsing E major rhythm, and the song breaks loose with an energetic, up-tempo rhythm.

Following this complex, almost 'proggy' introduction, lyrically 'Blue Eyed Lady' isn't anything special. A girl is at a gig alone and seems to be lonely. She starts out on her own, and continues to remain seated whilst the band are 'really moving' and 'everyone is grooving around'. There is a brief reprise of the second part of the introduction before the story resumes, 'The party's nearly over, your eyes still read the same, are you looking for someone who never came?'

The fourth verse reveals that nothing has happened; she's still there, apparently miserable. There is a repeat of the third section of the introduction before we're off to the races with Rossi throwing in another effortlessly melodic solo as Andy Bown bangs his ivories for all he's worth. The song goes into a long fade without a resolution to the slight tale, but that doesn't matter with all the energy and tight playing which is the focal point of the number. The song would be a surprise and welcome inclusion in the set-lists for the 2013 and 2014 Frantic Four reunion tours.

'Caroline' (Rossi/Young) Duration: 4.17 Chord Count: 8

This wonder is right up there with 'Down Down', 'Rocking All Over The World', and 'Whatever You Want' as one of Quo's most famous songs. 'Caroline' was released as a single in slightly abridged form and was backed with 'Joanne' which was recorded at the same time as the rest of *Hello!*, but not included on the album.

Kicking off with Parfitt's relentless high energy rhythm playing, Rossi unleashes the famous 'Police Siren' guitar melody, and Lancaster and Coghlan power their collective way forward with simple but supremely effective contributions. The familiar full guitar melody runs through its twelve-bar sequence twice, the second time being even heavier than the first, before the first verse.

Lyrically, of course, it's nothing special. Critics were quick to jump on the repetitive phrases, easy rhymes, and general sense of meaninglessness in some of the band's songs. But, as Rossi said in ...*XS-All Areas*;

> Putting 'meaning' into the lyrics was never top of my agenda when it came to writing a song. The tune was everything, and the words would be written to fit in with it, not the other way around.

It's the combination of the melody, harmony vocals, and grinding rhythm playing that make 'Caroline' so special. There is a clever musical device inserted under the chorus words '*Come on s*weet Caroline'; the tonic F chord has a low E note briefly inserted before hammering on back to an F. This motif is used wherever the tonic chord appears in the chorus. It's not new; Eddie Cochran used it in 'Summertime Blues' and 'C'mon Everybody', but that does nothing to reduce its effect here.

The solo is 'that tune again' which is followed by four bars of straight rhythm before the final verse and chorus. There is a quieter reprise of the guitar melody before the recording levels hit red once more as the melody is played through two further times, growing in intensity until coming to a sudden, dramatic halt with a quick descending bass melody rounding things off. 'Caroline' quickly became a timeless classic and justifiably so, it captures the joyfully optimistic spirit of early rock and roll, and places it firmly inside a sensational hard rock groove.

'Softer Ride' (Lancaster/Parfitt) Duration: 4.00 Chord Count: 3

Recorded during the sessions for *Piledriver*, and released as the B-side to 'Paper Plane', 'Softer Ride' ended up on *Hello!* as the band found they were a song short of the album's required running length.

Built around a hypnotic octave A shuffle riff, and a repeated descending major pentatonic run, 'Softer Ride' is the first song on the album to show any significant dynamic variation since 'Roll Over Lay Down'. The verse vocal refrain, 'I ain't gonna work, I ain't gonna work no more' is harmonised, and at 0.58, the rest of the band crash in with a magnificent revolving minim triplet chromatic riff which is played three times. A familiar upbeat rhythm comes in under the octave pentatonic riff, and the song lifts into its second chord for 'I could go back to the job I had, but the same old thing only drives me mad' before the pentatonic scale under the refrain, and a climatic 'Never again will I have to be ... down'.

Rossi's solo (2.17-2.41) is jaunty and tuneful, climaxing in a chromatic run and a repeat of the pentatonic tune. The volume drops down for the refrain, the pentatonic riff coming in at full strength, and another solo takes flight. The coda section has a short descending melody played in unison and octaves from all three guitarists before the song ends on the flattened seventh interval.

'Softer Ride' is an overlooked jewel of early Quo compositions. It has melody, harmony, power, clever arrangements, excellent playing, and shows just how creative the band could be within the relatively restricted world of 'just three chords'.

'And It's Better Now' (Rossi/Young) Duration: 3.18 Chord Count: 3

'And It's Better Now' is the album's second uplifting song with a religious theme. The album's only ballad is more of a power-pop song, a beautifully arranged melodic number with great interplay between the guitars.

The song is only a ballad for the introduction and the verses. There is a highly effective phase modulation effect applied to the vocals, and Lancaster mimics this melody an octave down. This type of subtle, inventive arrangement adds much to the effect of this musical oasis.

When the anthemic, uplifting chorus commences, we're back to full bore Quo, but with an increased emphasis on melody and harmony. This is most evident in the instrumental section (2.16-2.44), where Rossi, Parfitt and Lancaster play a trio melody built around a straightforward major key melody; the song is in F sharp, dangerous territory for the inexperienced guitarist. Clever uses of rests (the silences between the notes) as musical space make this all the more effective. The final choruses are exuberant and uplifting, with a brief 'guitars only' riff bringing this excellent number to a tight close.

'Forty Five Hundred Times' (Rossi/Parfitt) Duration: 9.52 Chord Count: 5

'Forty Five Hundred Times' is two songs glued together with some impressive extended instrumental creativity. The longest track on the album, or indeed *any* Quo studio album, the number ended up being lengthened even further when it was played live. In a radio interview in April 1982, Parfitt commented:

I always remember when we actually recorded it. It started off, it was written as a three to four-minute piece, which turned into a track of nearly ten minutes long and this happened because we used to record much as we're sitting now. In a tight circle on chairs with all the amplification around us, I mean the sound was ... I mean we were at stage volume, and it was a nightmare to try and mix it. But I always remember we got so off on one another and the last seven minutes ... on record are more or less ad-libbed, nobody quite knew what they were doing, but as I say we were getting so off on it, it just went on... '

'Forty Five Hundred Times' delivers the goods on every listen. Starting with a very quiet guitar introduction, joined 30 seconds in with a strident, country-flavoured lead line, the first verse is Parfitt, his guitar (tuned to an unusual 'open' tuning, B, B, D, G, B, E, low to high), and a simple hi-hat cymbal on each beat.

Those who were worried that they might be in for nearly ten minutes of such introspection need not be concerned as the band explodes at 1.15 for the second verse. This is where the two saxophone players can be heard – just - their presence being more noticeable in the held D major chord after the second 'Be my friend' refrain. The third verse is a disappointing repeat of the first but is massively enhanced by the full rock backing, and at 2.31, the huge chorus appears with Parfitt and Rossi singing in unison.

At 3.41, there is a fabulous instrumental section, a duet between Rossi and Lancaster. Played an octave apart for the vast majority of its eight-bar duration, it's fast, melodic, and a superb demonstration of the band's musicality. It's not easy to play on guitar, but for a bass player, it's an even bigger challenge, and Lancaster handles his lines with aplomb.

Rossi solos melodically over the relentless straight four beat drive which follows, and moves cleverly into a shuffle rhythm at 4.43. A brief period of purely rhythm section playing heralds in the second song at 5.08, 'I sure want to stay here, it sure feels fine...' with the vocals again sung in unison by Rossi and Parfitt. This is concluded less than 30 seconds later, and the remainder of the song is purely instrumental.

The feel moves from the shuffle rhythm back into a straight four beat around 6.10, with the tempo increasing substantially. The volume reduces around 7.18 as Parfitt gives his hands a rest, and piano and bass move to the foreground of the mix. Parfitt's back a minute later as Rossi goes off for a brief tea break before he rejoins the fray just before the nine-minute mark, adding more melodies around Lancaster's short phrases. The song begins to fade and, just as it's about to disappear, the constant, underlying B major chord suddenly lifts to an E before it's all over. It would have been fascinating to hear the 'full' version of this section to see what else the band managed to seemingly conjure up out of thin studio air.

Non Album Track
'Joanne' (Lancaster) Duration: 4.05 Chord Count: 9

Oh dear. The B-side to 'Caroline' is a disappointment. Where to begin?

Well, the introduction is twee, full of pretty harmonised guitars, like a castrated Thin Lizzy, and sounding like it's been imported from a 1960s pop song. There is also a prominent acoustic guitar throughout the song, which quickly outstays its welcome.

The verse is pleasingly chuggy and the refrain, 'Oh Joanne, I love you still' is reasonably melodic. However, Rossi's distinctive vocals sounds like he has been recorded down a telephone line, and a short repeated upper register guitar melody is given equal sonic billing in the mix. Lyrically it's a typical 'relationship over, I'm sad' dirge, and the music takes a truly bizarre turn for the instrumental section (2.34-3.02), where it resembles a 1960s surf band playing in Liverpool's famous Cavern Club. This is swamped with reverberation, but not enough to stop the guitar melody *really* getting on the nerves. The fourth verse is a repeat of the third, and the song goes into a mercifully quick fade as the first verse is reprised just to compound the boredom.

But 'Joanne', like 'Claudie', showed that a pop sensibility was tugging at the band's coat-tails, and these two songs reveal the undercurrents which would gradually rise to equal prominence with the band's hard-rocking roots.

Quo

Personnel:
Francis Rossi
Richard Parfitt
Alan Lancaster
John Coghlan
Guest musicians:
Bob Young: harmonica
Tom Parker: piano
Produced by Status Quo
Damon Lyon-Shaw: engineer
Richard Mainwaring: assistant engineer
Andy Miller: assistant engineer
Mixed by Damon Lyon-Shaw
Recorded at IBC Studios, London
Released on 18 May 1974
Highest chart position: 2
Weeks on chart: 16

In the spring of 1974, Quo returned to the studio to record their third album for Vertigo in less than three years. Retaining the same team and set-up (concert volume, and hang the complaints), the new vinyl was going to be called 'Quo Now', somehow becoming shortened along the way. In March 1974, responding to the ever-present criticism from the music press, Rossi said:

> Some people have this thing about the music being very samey, and it is in that we play mostly riffs. But anybody who has really listened notices lots of changes in feel. The band has a very recognisable style, but it goes deeper than that. We're very much a band to be listened to. I'm happy with the way the new album is going though there's bound to be people saying it's the same old stuff. That's their problem, though, because people who listen can tell different.

This is a continuation of the band's struggle with the media for acceptance as serious musicians since the release of 'Down The Dustpipe'. For the fans, of course, Quo were already the real deal. With *Quo,* more care was applied in the studio, and overall the compositions are crafted to be, in the main, more sophisticated and involving.

Quo's visuals are the brown to *Hello!'s* black. The concept of the sleeve was credited to Christine Patient, with design by 'Status Quo and Logo'. 'Logo' was actually Dave Field, an experienced album cover artist. He was responsible for the 'Tree of Quo Heads' black and white drawing where the roots tangle above ground to spell out the album title. The background resembles one of Roger Dean's fantastical landscapes which were used to great effect as album covers for prog-rockers Yes during the same period. The 'none-more-brown' theme is continued on the rear of the single sleeve cover, with the relevant information printed in gold. Inside was a foldout poster of the band in action on stage with the song lyrics printed on the reverse. Peculiarly, whilst the four members are listed, there is no instrumental association.

Quo is another 'dark' sounding album. There is too much reverb in the mix, and the balance of song writing has swung in favour of Parfitt and Lancaster, who provided five of the eight tracks. Rossi and Young contributed two songs, whilst 'Break the Rules' is the only song credited to all four members and Bob Young. *Quo* is, at times, spectacularly heavy. Lighter moments exist with the Rossi/Young compositions, and the multi-layered power ballad 'Lonely Man', but the album is definitely skewed towards the more brutal side of rock than its predecessors. Speaking in 2016, Rossi said:

> There was a period at that point, I was going to do a solo album, Bob and I were going to write countryish stuff. Alan and Rick took me to one side and said, 'We don't think you should be doing that, we don't think you're focusing enough on the band'. Up to that point, Bob and I had written everything, so they got together basically and wrote most of the Quo album. And to me, that one went too far 'that way'. There is some really good stuff on it, but there is some not-so-good stuff. It wasn't my fave album, because I felt like I was being manipulated too much at that point.

The origins of the split a decade later can be heard in *Quo*, and the singer's comments. By 1974 Rossi and Young were a successful song writing duo, and much credit for the band's chart success should be laid at their door. Lancaster preferred the band's heavier sound, although he could also write more sensitive songs. Parfitt, despite an early career on the cabaret circuit, was already living up to the Rock Star image, and enjoyed the *sturm und drang* sound more than the lighter moments. He too was capable of subtlety, but it wasn't his natural musical home. Things would improve with the next two albums. *On The Level* and, especially, *Blue For You* showed the band growing in all directions. After the high point of *Live*, however, the familiar, potent combination of drugs, alcohol, and growing musical differences meant that an unravelling was predictable and, with the benefit of hindsight, inevitable.

Quo is an unbalanced album. At times ('Drifting Away' and 'Don't Think It Matters') it's almost *too* heavy. 'Break The Rules' and especially 'Fine, Fine, Fine' have too much country influence in their good-time upbeat sound. 'Lonely Man' is a fine ballad which, whilst still having plenty of power behind it, sounds out of place. Reassuringly 'Backwater' and 'Just Take Me' showed that the band were still capable of producing the expected goods in different and interesting ways, whilst 'Slow Train' is another excellent album closer, better constructed and arranged than 'Forty Five Hundred Times'.

'Backwater' (Parfitt/Lancaster) Duration: 4.18 Chord Count: 8

'Backwater' is a great opener; a song that moves through three different keys, has dynamic contrast, and five distinct sections, all propelled by a great rocking groove and excellent musicianship.

The song starts with an urgent-sounding, minor key guitar riff played by Parfitt. Here he uses the same tuning as utilised for 'Forty Five Hundred Times' (a clever passing of the musical baton between albums) over two bars of 4/4 time. Rossi and Lancaster provide a major third harmony in the subsequent 2/4 bar. Parfitt's riff continues for three more bars of 4/4. This section is repeated with Lancaster's solid crotchet beat underneath Coghlan's highly aggressive drumming. Thirty-five seconds in the riff tumbles into a quieter section of arpeggiated guitar chords, with a sustained keyboard in the background. There is a gradual growth in volume until the music bursts into an archetypal Quo boogie at 1.08, with Rossi's off-beat chord stabs against Parfitt's solid rhythmic power. Again the use of the light and shade of good dynamic control is extremely effective.

Lancaster takes the lead vocals in this tale of a romantic rendezvous gone wrong, and the song pulsates like a well-oiled engine. At 2.40, a new section begins, 'What you looking for? What you looking for? Lady, do you know what you're looking for?' under which Coghlan's tribal drum rhythms sound suitably menacing. 'Backwater' moves into an instrumental with a rising chord sequence in a new key over which Rossi plays a magnificently melodic solo. The final verse kicks in at 3.48 with the song segueing smoothly into 'Just Take Me' with the power-chord punctuated lines 'I was *cold* when she left me, down the Backwater Road...'

'Just Take Me' (Parfitt/Lancaster) Duration: 3.34 Chord Count: 7

...and Coghlan's thunderous drumming takes over. This is the first Quo song to feature a lengthy drum and cowbell introduction, and there are other creative elements. Lancaster sings the first verse over Coghlan's backing, with no added instrumentation. A chromatic, rising chord sequence leads into the titular chorus lyrics, and then a funky staccato riff, played by Parfitt, joins the sonic backbone of the song. The rest of the band piles in for the second and third verses, and it is a wondrous noise, strong, controlled, and aggressive, with everyone sounding at the top of their game.

A new section is introduced at 1.30, featuring brief power chords interspersed with Coghlan's powerful playing. This is repeated four times before a brief drum fill leads into Rossi's spiky melodic solo, which, again, is just backed by Coghlan initially. Parfitt's funky riff joins in, and Rossi borrows a rising melody from the duet solo in 'Forty Five Hundred Times' at 2.31. The solo moves into a low register churning riff which blasts into the final verse, being a disappointing repeat of the first verse. The chorus refrain occurs three times before a tightly rhythmic ending to this unusual, inventive, and refreshingly new type of head-banger.

When performed live, 'Backwater' and 'Just Take Me' would be played in this 'through-style', becoming a single piece of music featuring two entirely different but equally satisfying rockers.

'Break The Rules' (Rossi/Young/Parfitt/Lancaster/Young) Duration: 3.37 Chord Count: 5

Released as the only single from the album, on 26 April 1974, backed with the non-album track 'Lonely Night', this is Quo returning to more traditional territory. All the familiar features are present and correct; Rossi's laconic, nasal delivery of an entertainingly shallow story, a solid shuffle rhythm, and a catchy refrain, 'Everybody has to sometimes break the rules'. Both musically and lyrically, it's Quo in a predictable pattern; there are two verses, a three-section instrumental, a third and fourth verse concluding the tale of a bar-room assignation gone wrong, and a slowed down, bluesy ending.

There is nothing *wrong* with 'Break The Rules'. Fans clearly agreed, pushing the single to number eight in the charts. But it's a step down from 'Caroline', lacking its predecessor's persuasive melodies and all-conquering powerful rhythms. The instrumental section (1.16-2.20) is the most musically interesting part. The first twelve-bar progression has a typical Rossi solo, the second part is a joyful, honky-tonk piano break, whilst Bob Young takes up the final third with some fine wailing harmonica playing over the powerhouse rhythmic accompaniment.

The *problem* with 'Break The Rules' is that there is no harmonic or dynamic variation throughout its duration. The verses and the instrumental section stick to the same chord sequence and, whilst there are some interesting arrangements with harmony guitar lines and piano and harmonica adding to the texture, the overall effect is one of relentless repetition. The invention and creativity, which marked out 'Backwater' and 'Just Take Me', is lacking here and there's a sense of uninspired familiarity about the track. 'Break The Rules' is in no way a *bad* song; it just lacks the spark and charisma of what preceded it.

'Drifting Away' (Parfitt/Lancaster) Duration: 5.02 Chord Count: 6

Fast, heavy, and relentless, 'Drifting Away' is the closest Quo come to outright heavy metal in this assault on the ears, although it virtually ties for this title with the equally pulverising 'Don't Think It Matters'.

The main riff is based around a descending minor pentatonic scale with a diminished fifth interval giving it the feel of an early 'blues-meets metal' Black Sabbath track. Once the rhythm kicks in, Parfitt sets forth on a brisk quaver D5 and D6 rhythm, whilst Rossi punctuates the drive with alternating D minor seventh and D seventh suspended fourth chords.

Lancaster's vocals are breathlessly urgent, and the whole song has an undeniable power running through it. After two dense, intense verses, there is an instrumental section commencing at 2.03 with some descending triplets, which leads bizarrely into an underpowered, major key country flavoured solo with harmonised guitars. The sonic fury returns for the main solo section (2.28-3.04), which powers into a third verse, and the coda section (4.40 onwards) reprises Rossi's solo section from 2.28 to a fade.

'Don't Think It Matters' (Parfitt/Lancaster) Duration: 4.51 Chord Count: 5

Go to your shed. Pick up the nearest hammer. Hit yourself repeatedly around the head with it for about five minutes. Congratulations. You have just recreated the 'Don't Think It Matters' listening experience.

Built around an insistent riff played in parallel fourths in the guitar's mid-range, this song has another overwhelmingly heavy underlying drive. What *just* places it at the number one slot in 'The Heaviest Track On The Album' stakes is the inventive use of rests and subtle changes in time signature in the instrumental section. Again, Lancaster handles the vocals with his characteristically gruff rock voice, and the chorus, which benefits from backing vocals, is simultaneously powerful and catchy.

At 1.41, the riff drops down into A major, returns to D, and then goes back to A before a typically reliable Rossi solo. At 2.23, a shout of exultation can just be heard above the stage volume recording as someone gets overwhelmed by the power of this impressive groove.

At 2.59, invention raises its head again. The third verse could just be sung with the same backing as before. Instead, Lancaster's raspy tone stands alone, 'Maybe I'm right..'... two harmonised power chords puncture the silence. '... or maybe I'm wrong'... two more, 'I just do the best that I *can*'. On 'can', the guitars play a descending minor pentatonic scale with a diminished fifth interval. It's the same idea as was used in 'Drifting Away', but it works just as effectively here, being played in triplets rather than the previous straight quaver rhythm. The staccato motif is repeated under the next lines, 'I'm working all night...', (power chords) 'you know I've worked through the night..., (power chords) woman can't you under*stand?*'

Further creativity is in evidence at 3.14, where the opening riff is played by all three guitarists with precise backing from Coghlan. Rather than play the riff over repeated bars of 4/4, the band slip in a bar of 2/4 after the third 4/4 bar as the riff slides from D into G. This trick is repeated as the riff moves back to D which then slides chromatically down to a sustained A major. Feedback starts to build, and then the full opening onslaught is repeated until a final chorus. The riff grooves away, alternating between D major and A major to a fade. It's magnificent, well-executed, and mind-numbing – at the right volume!

'Fine Fine Fine' (Rossi/Young) Duration: 2.29 Chord Count: 7

Nothing emphasises the gulf in writing styles between Parfitt/Lancaster and Rossi/Young at this point in Quo's history than this song coming directly after the previous crushing riffage.

'Fine Fine Fine' is a fast, upbeat, country rock number with a fantastically catchy sing-a-long chorus, plenty of nifty guitar playing, and a Mid-West American feel to the lyrics, 'My mama taught me how to read from the good book, my papa taught me how to win and lose the game'. You can almost hear the chair rocking on the porch as the coyotes howl in the distance, the evening wind gathering dust from the plain as the sunset throws the nearby cactuses into sharp silhouette. It's a bit less effective on a cold winter's day in a rain-sodden East Midlands town.

The majority of Rossi/Young songs were written on acoustic guitars and it shows here. 'Fine Fine Fine' would work better as a traditional country song rather than trying to mix in elements of rock at too fast a tempo. But as a diversion away from the heavy Parfitt/Lancaster bias of the album, it works well, and, by being the shortest number of the collection, doesn't outstay its welcome.

'Lonely Man' (Parfitt/Lancaster) Duration: 5.06 Chord Count: 7

This is the outlier in the *Quo* soundscape. Neither unrelentingly heavy or country boogie rock fun, 'Lonely Man' is a continuation of the style, established with 'All The Reasons' and 'And It's Better Now', of inserting a ballad as the penultimate number before an epic final track.

'Lonely Man' is an altogether more considered and constructed composition. Whilst the underlying chord sequences are straightforward, the layers of guitar melody and harmonies give the song a sense of grandeur which, thus far, has not been a hallmark of a Quo song. At times the song displays an almost 'Queen-like' sense of scope and ambition.

Parfitt and Lancaster finally unveil the more introspective side of their song writing skills. Opening with some atmospheric, strummed acoustic guitar, Parfitt takes the lead vocals for the only time on the album. The lyrics are thoughtful and receive a respectful musical arrangement, with plenty of harmonic interplay between the guitars. The second verse builds with bass, drums, and arpeggiated electric guitars, with the tension growing further into the bridge section (1.59-2.16) where a sustained organ adds to the texture.

A return to relative peace follows for the instrumental section with Rossi playing an understated melodic solo, and at 2.48, the band are unleashed with the lead lines flying high above the intense accompaniment. A ghostly vocal repeat of the bridge blends with Rossi's solo before the final verse, which moves into a quieter section, 'A friend is what you need, would you mind if it was me, maybe then you'll find what you were looking for'. The music builds again into an exultant, uplifting instrumental (4.07-4.53) followed by a short, quiet coda with a repeat of the 'Maybe then you'll find what you were looking for' line as the song finishes with a slow guitar arpeggio.

'Lonely Man' is another fine example of the breadth of song writing Quo could turn their hands to. There is a strong emphasis on melody, harmony, arrangement, and dynamics which combine to make this the most impressive of the 'pre-epic' ballad trio.

'Slow Train' (Rossi/Young) Duration: 7.52 Chord Count: 8

'Slow Train' is the band's best long song, packed with variation and interest whilst still maintaining a strongly rocking core. Essentially it is two separate numbers and a complex instrumental section joined to form a single, substantial piece of music, 'Slow Train' is structured, carefully arranged, well-performed, and shows yet again how creative and innovative Quo could be within the relative restraints of the rock and blues genres.

Starting in E major, a brisk up-beat shuffle rhythm sets the decidedly American tone of the song, 'I can't afford a ticket on an old Dakota airplane, I gotta jump a ride on a cattle truckin' slow train, I guess it doesn't matter as long as I can get my head down in the sun'. The second verse is heavier and the song lifts up to a new section where the intensity continues as Coghlan gets really busy with his cymbals, 'Hey mama, please now don't you fret none, don't worry but please don't you forget…'. The second half of this section has the band at full bore before a tight triplet-based ending.

This moves the music into its next phase with involved interplay between the guitars, and Lancaster playing melodic lines before a driving rhythm takes hold. Then the second song takes off, 'I came here in the morning and I crept out in the middle of night…'. The underlying chord progression here is the same as the opening verses of the track, but it feels like a completely different song. The vocals are harmonised and the entire section rocks along superbly.

At 3.01, a new instrumental section begins, initially with Lancaster again prominent, before Rossi takes a sixteen-bar solo. There is then a reprise of the bass-heavy bars, the tempo slows as the guitars play off each other, and a Celtic style jig emerges. Coghlan supplies some brisk military-style drumming as the tune is repeated and harmonised, with Lancaster's tuneful bass being an integral part of the arrangement. A new melody is played over descending chords before the jig comes around again, the entire section being concluded with just Rossi and Parfitt playing a new harmonised melody which gets faster and faster. This is reminiscent of the ending of the equally impressive instrumental section of 'Someone's Learning', where the guitars are a tight musical unit, rather than indulging the fashion for extended, meandering, and ultimately pointless solos. (Yes, Jimmy, I'm looking at you.) A mighty power chord leads into another thunderous example of Coghlan's drumming skills.

This also underlines the fact that the band clearly didn't have an effective way of merging the instrumental to the reprise of the opening verses (although these are now played in A major, which has been the dominant key since 1.51). A long triplet-based drum roll leads back into a reprise of the opening, which sounds just mighty, as Rossi's voice rides high above the band, giving it their all. The chorus refrain 'I guess it doesn't matter as long as I can get my head down in the sun', is repeated three times before a typically bluesy turnaround and a single power chord ending.

Blending a relatively simple form with clever arrangements, intricate playing and a *joie de vivre* performance, 'Slow Train' still sounds melodic and powerful decades later and is a further example of Quo at their very best.

Non-Album Track:
'Lonely Night' (Rossi/Parfitt/Lancaster/Coghlan) Duration: 3.23
Chord Count: 3
Roll call time! Major key, up-beat country rock feel? Check. Nasal vocals? Check. 'Get Back' style drumming rhythm? Check.

'Lonely Night' sounds like it can only have come from the Rossi/Young song writing stable, and yet, on the 2015 CD re-issue of *Quo*, it is credited to the entire band. Another source suggests Bob Young had a hand in it, and elsewhere that Coghlan did not. The joint writing credit may have been a 'royalty-share' situation, which were used to keep the less prolific writers in the band happy. It's hard to believe that it took four or five people to write this piece of light rock, but 'Break the Rules' exists on this basis, so who knows?

That said, 'Lonely Night' is a happy bouncing slice of boogie with more than a hint of country about it. Highly melodic and foot-tappingly cheerful, the second verse is harmonised and the refrain, 'No I never thought I'd see you here again' is memorable. There is a great little guitar and bass duet (2.06-2.22) after the second chorus, and the song fades out on repeated chorus refrains. As B-sides go, it's better than 'Joanne', but it's definitely no 'Softer Ride'. An enjoyable slice of driving pop-rock music, it was, nevertheless, the correct decision to omit this song from the album.

On The Level

Personnel:
Francis Rossi
Richard Parfitt
Alan Lancaster
John Coghlan
Guest musicians:
Bob Young: harmonica (uncredited)
Andy Bown: piano (uncredited)
Produced by Status Quo
Damon Lyon-Shaw: production assistant and engineer
Hugh Jones: engineer
Andy Miller: second engineer
Mixed by Damon Lyon-Shaw
Recorded at IBC Studios, and Phonogram Studios, London
Released on 1 March 1975
Highest chart position: 1
Weeks on chart: 27

In-between *Quo* and *On The Level*, the band left Gaff Management and joined manager Colin Johnson's new company, Quarry Productions. In the autumn of 1974, Quo returned to the studio to work on tracks for their next album. The writing and sound imbalance which had permeated *Quo* was redressed this time around with four songs being provided by Rossi and Young, one from Parfitt and Young, two written by Parfitt, and a single contribution from Lancaster. For the first time since *Piledriver*, a crowd-pleasing cover version was included, this being a rip-roaring version of Chuck Berry's 'Bye Bye Johnny'.

As a taster of what was to come, Phonogram, Vertigo's parent company, released a shortened version of 'Down Down' as a single. Within six weeks, the song was at number one, the first of 1975, and, by the end of February, *On The Level* had mirrored this success, becoming their second album to reach the top spot. This also led its predecessors to sell to a new and growing audience; *Piledriver, Hello!,* and *Quo* all returned to the charts.

The album cover is impressive. Shot in an Ames room (an interior which creates an optical illusion), it showed Parfitt (too good looking to exist in a fair and just universe), and Coghlan (from a distance almost feminine, if you overlook the big droopy moustache) in the background to the left. To the right and forward in shot is an oversized Lancaster, and kneeling front and centre, Rossi is resplendent in what had become his trademark look, the denim jeans, white tee-shirt and waistcoat combo. Opening up the gatefold sleeve revealed many small photos of the band and crew enjoying 'down-time' at a variety of places whilst on tour. Inside the sleeve, the dust cover for the vinyl had the song lyrics printed in blue on a white background. On the rear of the sleeve, the Ames Room is reprised, left to right we have smaller versions of Lancaster and Rossi, in the middle is Parfitt, and an inflated Coghlan occupies the right hand side.

The bright colours of the packaging are matched by the sound of the album. Gone is the doomy reverb which had drenched much of *Hello!* and *Quo*. Here the band sounds alive, pulsating, and full of energy. There is a mixture of out and out rockers mixed with some relatively lighter compositions. And, of course, audience favourites 'Down Down' and 'Bye Bye Johnny' kept heads banging and hands clapping. *On The Level* did, however, also serve as a turning point for the band's writing. Only two of its ten tracks exceeded five minutes, whilst the rest all sit tidily within the three or four-minute mark. The focus here is on concise, melodic, yet still powerful tracks. Although *On The Level* is a rebalancing of the group dynamic, it didn't affect the drive and ambition of the individual members. Lancaster saw the album as a complete contrast to *Quo*; 'It had swung back the other way', he is quoted as saying in the inlay booklet for the 2016 CD reissue of the album

We were still very much together, headspace-wise. That's the difference between a band and a group of musicians. All of us were so in tune we knew intuitively where the arrangements would go. Songs were sometimes left half-finished to be worked out in the studio, where the sparks really flew.

Rossi's view, from the same sleeve notes was;

Quo felt a bit weird to me. Rick and Nuff (Lancaster), mainly Nuff, had felt they had their thing going with *Quo*, which they wanted to be more fist-in-the-air. With *On The Level* we got back more of the MOR pop element, which I've always felt suited us far better.

And in that final sentence Rossi, maybe unwittingly, draws back the veil on the incoming divergence in sound and style which would beset Quo from 1977 onwards. With Lancaster as the out and out hard rocker, and Parfitt somewhere in between the rock and a country place, it would increasingly be Rossi's more melodic, pop-based instincts which would come to dominate and define the 'Frantic Four Sound'. He went on to conclude that *On The Level* was his favourite album of the era:

In *On The Level* we seemed to have a beautiful mix of the frantic rocking thing and a bit of pop content. People turn their noses up at pop music, but what do you think it all is? It's just popular music, and we're just lucky it's popular!

To celebrate Quo's thirteenth anniversary, an EP single was issued on 13 May 1975. This featured 'Roll Over Lay Down', recorded live at The Kursaal, Southend, a new studio version of 'Gerdundula', and 'Junior's Wailing' live at

Trentham Gardens, Stoke. The EP rose to number nine in the singles chart and was included on the 2016 reissue of *On The Level* along with the single edit of 'Down Down', and live recordings of 'Roadhouse Blues', Backwater', 'Just Take Me', 'Claudie', 'Little Lady', 'Most Of The Time', and 'Bye Bye Johnny'. At this stage in their career, it seemed as if Quo could do no wrong. That would all change two years and one album later.

'Little Lady' (Parfitt) Duration: 3.02 Chord Count: 3
'Little Lady' explodes out of the speakers with a breathless energy. Opening with the refrain melody of 'I was like a rollin' stone' played three times, the underlying dominant seventh chord, an F sharp, is sustained, the simple act of adding in the major third interval fires the starting gun, and we're off.

It's joyously noisy. Parfitt sings his own composition, another 'relationship gone south' song, with conviction. As usual with Quo numbers, the lyrics are secondary to the music, although the chorus is compelling, 'Found myself all alone, ain't no fun on your own, now I'm like a rolling stone'. The second verse is harmonised, and the subsequent instrumental section takes off with a 'rise and fall' melody in the mid-range of the guitar, a repeat of the introduction, and an unexpected 180 degree turn into a calmer section (1.20-1.43) where the music modulates from B to F sharp major.

Rossi plays a very pretty melodic descending chromatic melody against Parfitt's arpeggios, with Coghlan decorating the space with a hi-hat beat and occasional subtle cymbals. The underlying harmony moves to B major and Lancaster joins in with root notes played on the off beat as Coghlan increases his contribution. The music drops back to F sharp and then into E major, beginning to grow in volume and ferocity, back up to F sharp and leading into a furious solo over a hard driving rhythm. The final section of the instrumental has Parfitt staying on the dominant seventh as Lancaster moves down the scale underneath him, increasing the expectation of the third verse. This is the power of dynamic, melodic control writ (and played) large; the closing third of the song sounds mighty due to the changes in volume and arrangement which have preceded it.

This final verse is also harmonised with the refrain turning into a sloweddown heavy rock ending, with Coghlan rolling around his kit as the chord slowly fades. 'Little Lady' sounds *so alive*, a fact that is neatly emphasised by the next track emerging from the dying away of its final chord…

'Most Of The Time' (Rossi/Young) Duration: 3.19 Chord Count: 5
Rossi's plaintiff, raspy vocal style signals the start of 'Most Of The Time' with the guitars playing effective arpeggios underneath his affecting melody. As with the *pianissimo* section of 'Little Lady', the guitar sound has had a gentle phased modulation effect added, giving a sparkle and shine to the music.

This opening section concludes with the lilting chorus until a bruising, fullon instrumental section, reminiscent of the third part of 'Railroad', crushes all in its path with a relentlessly heavy groove, as Rossi wrenches all manner of pain from his Telecaster. At 2.18, the vocals return over the heaviness with the sing-a-long refrain interspersed with Coghlan's distinctive round-the-kit rolls before coming to a live end.

A fade may have been preferable here, but the band clearly wanted to continue with the 'live-in-the-studio' feel. Like 'Backwater'/'Just Take Me' before it, 'Most Of The Time' would be usually played as a direct continuation of 'Little Lady' on stage.

'I Saw The Light' (Rossi/Young) Duration: 3.38 Chord Count: 4

There is another change of feel for the album's third track. The powerful blues rock of 'Little Lady' and the rolling heaviness of 'Most Of The Time' is now displaced in favour of a jaunty major key riff, and a brisk tempo. Rossi's reedy vocals review a now-dead relationship, where the couple seemed to be perpetually arguing until, finally, enough was enough. Again, the lyrics are subservient to the music.

Coghlan's drumming throughout the song is impressive. He knows how to hold down a groove and also when to drop in the occasional fill to add colour and interest. Lancaster and Parfitt keep the rhythm riveted together like the well-oiled machine they have become through years of gigging, whilst Rossi's vocals add a folk-tinged sparkle to the melodies, which have a pleasant pop feel to them.

There is a nice musical touch in the chorus. Whilst the chord sequence is G major followed by D major (before returning to the key of A major), the band slip in a semi-tone step below the G and D, giving the section an additional swing. It's subtle but effective and similar to the 'Cochran Trick' played in the chorus of 'Caroline'. 'I Saw The Light' is another gem of a Quo song; simple in structure yet highly melodic and rhythmically engaging. It's a long way away from being 'just another album track', and should have received greater promotion on stage. The exact same comments also apply to the following number.

'Over And Done' (Lancaster) Duration: 3.52 Chord Count: 3

Another song with a glistening commercial edge in its major key melody and quick, driving rhythm, 'Over And Done', continues the 'bad relationship/upbeat music' feel of 'I Saw The Light'.

There's an excellent, clean-sounding, aggressively strummed chord sequence before the bass and drums drop in, with a descent into a fast foot-tapper as a folk style guitar melody sits on top. Vocal harmonies join for the verse and chorus, although Rossi's voice has a rougher edge to it than in previous numbers. Pitch wise the song is, at times, at the upper end of his range.

There is a sprightly solo section again with Celtic influenced overtones before a reprise of the introduction with Lancaster's up and down bass slide leading into the final verse and chorus. A thrice-repeated refrain leads into a repeat of the second part of the introduction, and a clearly picked guitar coda.

Lancaster's contributions are usually harder edged than this, but 'Over And Done' works well. It would have been interesting to hear the bassist's gutsier vocal style handle his composition as, so far, we've had three back-to-back Rossi vocals. That is in no way a bad thing, but when you've got three talented singers and songwriters in a band, variety would add greater sonic spice to the overall mix.

'Nightride' (Parfitt/Young) Duration: 3.51 Chord Count: 4

Okay, this is the comparative dud in the collection. 'Nightride' is a droner, emphasised by the regular alternation of the D sharp in the B major and D natural in the subsequent E seventh chords, which dominate the song. The tempo feels flabby, lacking in the taut energy and sonic shine which has dominated the album's first four songs. If it was ten per cent faster, the song would be a much more engaging experience.

'Nightride' was the B-side to 'Down Down' when it was released as a single and seems to hark back to an earlier age of Quo. It wouldn't have sounded out of place on *Dog...* or *Piledriver*. It's heavy on the groove, and the verse vocals are well harmonised, but the lyrics don't stand close observation, and there is nothing by way of textural or dynamic variation to maintain interest. Rossi's solo has a 'by the book' feel to it and, whilst Coghlan sounds like he's enjoying himself hitting every drum and cymbal hard, there's a predictability to the music. It's outstayed its welcome by the time we get to the repeated 'You, you, you, you, you move me' coda, which takes *far* too long to fade.

'Down Down' (Rossi/Young) Duration: 5.22 Chord Count: 7

Guitar freaks, pay attention; Rossi's introduction cannot be played in 'standard' tuning. At the risk of alienating the non-playing reader, I should mention that Quo made a habit of using alternative tunings in a number of their songs. Parfitt, in particular, was fond of the B B D G B E variant, which he deployed to great effect on 'Forty Five Hundred Times', and would also unleash on 'Rain' the following year. For 'Down Down', Rossi detunes, going for G G D G B D, then placing a capo at the fourth fret, transporting the song, like 'Little Lady', 'Most Of The Time', and 'Nightride' before it, into the key of B major. Parfitt remains in a guitarists 'standard' (E A D G B E) tuning. Please wake up at the back; I'm onto the song now.

Lyrically 'Down Down' is another example of Quo's stance that it was the sound of the words rather than the words themselves which added to the overall quality and effect of a song. Rossi disputes any sexual connotation to the track, insisting that the verse lines 'I want all the world to see, to see you're laughing and you're laughing at me, I can take it all from you' were aimed both at the critical press, and obliquely to his then-wife.

'Down Down' gave the Frantic Four their only number one single. It's not hard to see why. The guitar shine has been re-polished, the track gleams with melodic invention, and the driving riff and bulldozing rhythm make for an overwhelming cocktail of sound. Rossi is back in fine voice and the rest of the band is super-tight throughout. There is no solo section as such; instead, we have an instrumental interlude (1.26-1.37) where Lancaster can be heard scuttling around busily behind Rossi and Parfitt's jangling guitars. A different chordal section (2.08-2.36) based around sustained and arpeggiated chords is played five times (four would be too obvious,) the final chord dying away with a 'wait-for-it' sense of anticipation. On stage, Rossi would milk this for all it was worth, before the infectious guitar rhythm starts up again, driving vigorously into a brief stop before another chorus/verse/chorus sequence.

There is a reprise of the second instrumental at 3.33, which is played three times, of course (four would be too many), and then we're into the extended coda section. This alternates between B major and E major chords, with Lancaster throwing in short upper range melodies, and Coghlan really going for it in the shed-building stakes. The bass rises up to its highest frets as what sounds like a tribute to Glen Miller's 'In The Mood' played to a straight quaver rather than swung rhythm takes hold, and this magnificent piece of music fades away.

'Broken Man' (Lancaster) Duration: 4.12 Chord Count: 6
Another Lancaster song with a great chordal groove running through it, 'Broken Man' sees the bassist take over lead vocal duties in this dispiriting tale of a man who's been released from jail and, having nothing else to do with his freedom, drinks his time away. It sounds like your classic recipe for a dirgey, minor key blues song, but 'Broken Man' is lively, melodic, and spirited. This is no more apparent than in the cheerfully sing-a-long refrain 'Drinking gets you nowhere, but nowhere's where I am, guess I'll always be a backstreet broken man'.

The joyful musical mood continues with the instrumental section, where Rossi's melodic soloing skills are brought to the fore. There is a great mid-section change of feel at 2.19, where the tempo slows, and Coghlan has some deep drum fills around the surrounding sustained chords. The intricate guitar introduction is reprised and soon drives into the final verse and chorus, with another live ending. 'Broken Man' is the third overlooked gem in this particular Quo goldmine.

'What To Do' (Rossi/Young) Duration: 2.50 Chord Count: 5
The chorus lyric features the phrase 'I didn't know just what to do' three times. I do. Press 'Next'.

This song sounds like it's related to 'I Saw The Light', but this one is the black sheep. There's a similar tempo and upbeat feel, a catchy vocal melody, and a major key brightness it, but 'What To Do' loses points by having little to contribute in the lyric department, and a *very* average chorus.

The introduction borrows its chord progression from Thin Lizzy's 'The Boys Are Back In Town', and overall the song sounds thrown together. It's bouncy and fun, like a Labrador puppy, but the track lacks staying power and sits alongside 'Nightride' in the second division of songs on the album.

The best part of the number is Rossi's solo as the song kicks up a key to B major (1.57-2.22), and whilst it's always a pleasure to listen to the band groove away, there isn't enough about the track to keep the ears enthralled. With further creativity and invention, 'What To Do' could have turned out to be the dark horse song of the album, but that would mean I'd have to find another animal-based metaphor to describe it, and that would probably fox me.

'Where I Am' (Parfitt) Duration: 2.45 Chord Count: 5

'Where I Am' is the album's seemingly obligatory ballad, played out against a soothing texture of twelve and six-string acoustic guitars with sustained keyboards and some effective choral backing vocals in the background. Coghlan is not involved, he may be resting up before the album's final track, and the overall effect of 'Where I Am' is of a little oasis of melodic tranquillity.

It's straightforward in the extreme, three verses, three choruses, interspersed with a steel-strung acoustic guitar solo that mimics the vocal melody. There is no bridge section, nor dynamic or textural changes, and whilst 'Where I Am' is an effective buffer between 'What To Do' and 'Bye Bye Johnny', that's all it is. Never mind the lyrics; bathe in the warm waters of this pretty song with Parfitt's vocals in restrained and heartfelt mode. It's the calm before the storm...

'Bye Bye Johnny' (Berry) Duration: 4.32 Chord Count: 4

Opening with Lancaster's shouted 'And here we go with fearful fingers...' and a swift count in as Coghlan performs a 'start your engines, gentlemen' drum roll, Rossi blasts out the introduction, and we are back in the land of *Piledriver* level intensity.

Lancaster handles the vocals convincingly against the high energy, wall-rattling backing, Rossi throws in a typically biting solo, and the entire song races along like it's very late for an urgent appointment. Dynamics, one of Quo's core arranging skills, is not overlooked, and at 2.34, the volume drops dramatically for three choruses with the lead guitar doodling away in the background. At 3.24, the recording levels suddenly hit the red again before a Rossi solo which mixes elements of Berry's style with his own melodic gifts. The song finishes on a single power chord and drum fill, after which the overdubbed sound of a crowd singing 'You'll Never Walk Alone' closes the album in an entirely appropriate way.

This was the final song in the musical 'Carousel', which also found favour with supporters of Liverpool Football Club. Here it becomes adopted by a similarly fanatical group of fans, the ultra-loyal and ever-growing Quo Army. Rodgers and Hammerstein would, no doubt, be very proud.

Blue For You

Personnel:
Francis Rossi
Richard Parfitt
Alan Lancaster
John Coghlan
Guest musicians:
Bob Young: harmonica
Andy Bown: piano
Produced by Status Quo
Damon Lyon-Shaw: co-producer and engineer
Hugh Jones: engineer
Andy Miller: second engineer
Mixed by Damon Lyon-Shaw
Recorded at Phonogram Studios, London
Released on 20 March 1976
Highest chart position: 1
Weeks on chart: 30

Blue For You saw a subtle change in the band's image. Gone were the semi-scruffy, second-hand clothes of the *Piledriver* era. Now the look was brand new, specifically tailored denim, a result of a huge advertising contract with the American corporate behemoth, Levi Strauss. It was an implicit acknowledgement of Quo's standing in the public eye that a company the size of Levi's saw them as a marketing opportunity. The front cover of the new album bore neither the band logo, nor the album title. Instead, there was a photograph of the Frantic Four looking distinctly un-frantic, more akin to a fashion shoot than a rock band. Image wise it seemed as if the band had re-embraced commercialism, although this time it was one of their own making.

Against a black background Rossi, Lancaster and Parfitt are standing, whilst Coghlan sits cross-legged on what looks suspiciously like a denim shag pile carpet, the drummer looking like he's been put on the naughty step. On the reverse of the original gatefold sleeve was the name and title in the familiar logo, this time coloured matching silver and black, above a truncated shot of the band showing just their waistlines. The inside of the sleeve showed Parfitt, Rossi, and Lancaster in their trademark 'attack stance', whilst Coghlan is in the background surrounded by an array of cymbals and amplifiers. The cover didn't even get as far as naming the band, or their instrument allocation. It was Quo, and that was all you needed to know. The song lyrics were included on the inner dust sleeve, printed silver on blue.

Another change was the recording location. In place of the familiar IBC studios, which had proved such a useful 'live stage' setting for their previous four albums, the band decamped to Phonogram Studios. Due to their increasing financial success and consequent tax issues, this was the last occasion they would record an album in the UK.

As a teaser for the new album 'Rain', backed with the non-album track 'You Lost The Love', was released as a single on 6 February 1976. It reached number seven in the chart. *Blue For You* went straight into the album charts at number one, their fifth consecutive album to reach the top three. It spent almost seven months in the charts, becoming the 28th best seller of 1976. In July, an edited version of 'Mystery Song', backed with, oddly, 'Drifting Away', was the second single and got to number eleven.

In December, the band's third '45 of the year, a cover of the old country and western song, 'Wild Side Of Life', landed at number nine. The B-side was another non-album track, 'All Through The Night'. This was the first time since their days with Pye that the band had gone into the studio specifically to record a single and use an outside producer, in this case, Deep Purple bassist, Roger Glover.

From the outside, everything was looking very rosy indeed. However, and possibly inevitability, drugs were beginning to play an increasing part in the band's life. Rossi takes up the story in his autobiography:

> Rick, Alan, and I were all doing a lot of coke by then. Not John. He was not into that at all. He was still into his beer. Boy, was he into his beer… (Rick and I) were both doing a fair bit of speed at that point, white amphetamine sulphate powder that looked much like coke and which you could also snort lines of. Speed, though, had a much more pronounced effect. At its best, it definitely aided creativity. When we were making the *Blue For You* album in 1976, Rick, Alan and I were all speeding out of our nuts night and day.

The album marks the end of an astonishingly creative era for Quo. Since signing to Vertigo, they had released five excellent albums that saw them both pushing the boundaries and re-defining the genres of twelve-bar and blues rock music. They had also enjoyed incredible success in the singles chart with six Top Twenty releases in the same period. Their fan base had expanded massively, assisted by an unrelenting gigging schedule.

Blue For You is the culmination of this hard work and talent. Both in its sound and song writing, the album is an immense piece of work. The band have distilled the best of their wide range of skills; there is power and energy in abundance, but there is also much creativity and melody, and new ideas are explored within a familiar framework. There's also a pleasing symmetry to the writing and track sequencing; going back to the days of vinyl, Lancaster/Rossi provided both side openers; Rossi and Young wrote the next track(s), with Lancaster providing two uncharacteristically softer songs. Parfitt finished off each side with a massive, magnificent hit single heads down rocker.

Blue For You captures the shine and energy of *On The Level*, the outright heaviness of *Quo*, the melodic skills of *Hello!* and, of course, the overwhelming

Right: The Pre-Frantic Four during their 'pop' era with Pye. Lancaster would later buy Rossi's moustache from him.

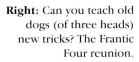

Left: Yes, we are having a lovely time on or holidays. Quo - circa 'Living On An Island'.

Right: Can you teach old dogs (of three heads) new tricks? The Frantic Four reunion.

Left: The first album. Appropriately enough, all copies should be placed on top of a mountain of matchsticks and let fate take its course. (*Pye*)

Right: The difficult (to listen to) second album. (*Pye*)

Left: After a couple of false starts, our story finally gets going with *Ma Kelly...* (*Pye*)

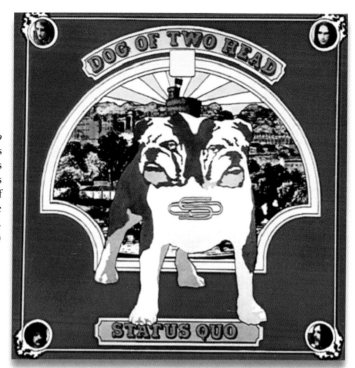

Right: *Dog Of Two Head*; 'serious music' from 'serious musicians'. There's some great stuff hidden within the truly awful cover. (*Pye*)

Left: *Piledriver*; The trademark 'attack stance'. An album that (almost) does exactly what it says on the tin. (*Vertigo*)

Left: An early TV appearance, featuring an extremely tall Bob Young on harmonica.

Right: From the same show, the final song before Lancaster had to leave for an emergency haircut.

Left: Roy Lynes, possibly playing in the 'saddest of all keys'.

Right: Bob Young gives it his all in front of a particularly unenthusiastic crowd.

Left: Rossi, with charisma chip fully engaged on *Top of the Pops* in 1973.

Right: Parfitt, just after spotting a rodent on the *Top of the Pops* studio floor.

Left: *Hello!;* the first Quo album to enter the charts at number one. (*Vertigo*)

Right: *Quo*; some very heavy rock meets some country (but luckily, no western). (*Vertigo*)

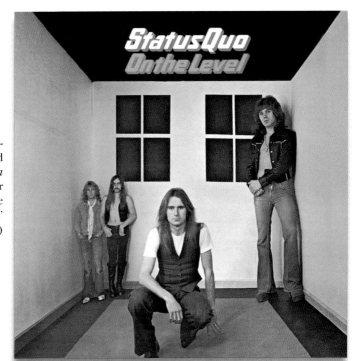

Right: The eye-bending and ear-marauding *On The Level*. Another 'straight to the top of the charts' release. (*Vertigo*)

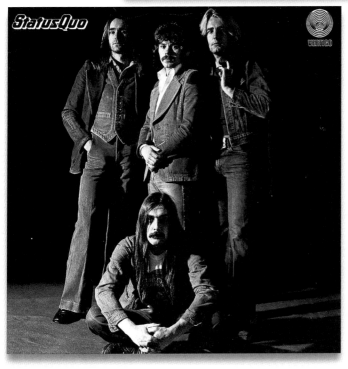

Left: *Blue For You*; the Norton Commando of Quo's 1970's output, and the high-water mark of their studio career. (*Vertigo*)

Left: Lancaster at Live Aid.

Right: The opening act at the world's biggest concert; Live Aid, 13th July 1985.

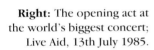

Left: Rossi at Live Aid; nice day for it..

Right: Parfitt at Live Aid. No, he's not playing a double-neck guitar – Rossi is playing hide and seek.

Left: Live Aid – The view from the Andy Bown part of the stage.

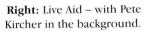

Right: Live Aid – with Pete Kircher in the background.

Left: *Rocking All Over The World.* Oh dear. (*Vertigo*)

Right: *Live* – a fine document of the band steamrolling the Glasgow Apollo. (*Vertigo*)

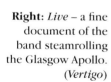

Right: *If You Can't Stand The Heat* – a better sounding album than its predecessor, but still far more filler than thriller. (*Vertigo*)

Left: *Whatever You Want* – the best album of the post-*Blue For You* era. (*Vertigo*)

Left: Nostalgia overload! The Frantic Four finally reunite.

Right: Lancaster at a reunion show, battling ill health but still going for it.

Left: Coghlan at a reunion show.

Right: Rossi cheering Coghlan up at a reunion show.

Left: The Frantic Four, in an uncharacteristically un-frantic shot.

Right: Rossi and Parfitt; still rocking after all those years.

Left: *Just Supposin'*; a good sound, but very few good songs. (*Vertigo*)

Right: *Never Too Late*; the very quick follow up with, perversely, better songs but poorer production. (*Vertigo*)

STATUS QUO
1982

Right: *1+8+9+2*; 'Happy Anniversary' Not. (*Vertigo*)

=

Left: *Back To Back*; The last time Lancaster would join Rossi and Parfitt in the studio. Terrible in every department. (*Vertigo*)

Left: *Live At The NEC;* The live album of the Prince's Trust concert – proving they've still got it, even in front of royalty. (*Vertigo*)

Right: The live album from the first of the reunion tours. (*Abbey Road*)

Left: The final night of the final tour of the Frantic Four. (*Abbey Road*)

power of *Piledriver*. At times incredibly fast, heavy and relentless, there is also space for good old-fashioned boogie, the slow blues of the title track, two classic rockers, and some surprises in the funk-laced 'That's A Fact' and the sly, jazzy-tinged shuffle of 'Ease Your Mind'.

Whilst critics of the album may say that it lacks the innovation of earlier albums (there is no 'Big Fat Mama' or Slow Train', for example), *Blue For You* scores with its cohesiveness. Polished and powerful, like a high-revving Norton Commando, the album is all-conquering. The compositions *still* sound fresh and inspired today, and the arrangements and playing are ferociously impressive. There's an overall feeling that the band's stars, whether chemically assisted or not, have all aligned. How do you follow that? Well, the short(ish) answer is they could have, should have, but didn't. Their next studio effort would be a very different proposition indeed.

12 March 1977 saw the release of the 'obligatory-for-the-decade' double live album, imaginatively titled *Live!* This was recorded over three nights at the Apollo Theatre in Glasgow on 27, 28 and 29 October 1976, with the majority of the songs being taken from the first performance.

The cover, the only one for them by legendary album sleeve creators Hipgnosis, had a live-action poster of the band torn to reveal a black and white posed shot of Rossi, Lancaster, Parfitt and Coghlan underneath. The designers were aiming for a juxtaposition that would avoid the typical 'band-on-stage' photos which adorned similar albums (think Thin Lizzy's *Live And Dangerous*, Rainbow *On Stage*, or both of Deep Purple's live releases.) Hipgnosis sought to recreate a street wall where posters had been pasted on top of each other. When one is ripped by fans, or the ravages of time, so another could be partially seen. This tearing was a decisive but spontaneous action, an appropriate reflection of a live performance. The overall effect is the eye sees enough of each partial image to recreate two complete pictures in the mind.

The inside of the gatefold sleeve had fifteen small photos of the timeline of one of the gigs superimposed over an exterior shot of the venue by night. The inner dust sleeves had, bizarrely, individual interior colour photos of the band, all smiling. Yes, even Coghlan. I know! Worryingly Rossi is wearing a jumper. I thought there were rules against that sort of thing. The track listing was:

'Junior's Wailing', 'Backwater', 'Just Take Me', 'Is There A Better Way', 'In My Chair', 'Little Lady', 'Most Of The Time', 'Rain', 'Forty Five Hundred Times', 'Roll Over Lay Down', 'Big Fat Mama', 'Don't Waste My Time', 'Roadhouse Blues', 'Caroline', 'Bye Bye Johnny'

Live! reached number three, spending a total of fourteen weeks in the charts. Rossi is of the opinion that it isn't a great recording, but it remains a firm favourite with the Quo Army fan base.

'Is There A Better Way' (Rossi/Lancaster) Duration: 3.27 Chord Count: 8

Quo's most explosive opening track is a masterpiece of concise writing, tight arrangement, adroit playing, and overwhelming power. Beginning with heavyweight power chords, the song soon hits a high-speed groove with energy, attitude, and real aggression. Lancaster handles the vocals with aplomb in this rare collaboration with Rossi.

At 0.58, the time switches to a rolling 6/8 time signature, and a more relaxed feel for the first instrumental, with Rossi supplying an elegant legato melody as choral style backing vocals fill out the texture. At 1.22, the introduction is reprised and, at 1.36, there is what sounds like a mistake as Coghlan hits his bass drum a beat too soon, just before the next chorus and verse take flight. This quickly leads into the magnificent second instrumental at 2.04, a descending power chord progression which is fast, heavy, and spectacular. At 2.34, the lead guitar returns with a melodic solo, amid choral harmonies, until the final lyrics and the song pounds away to a fade. And as with this point in 'Down Down', Lancaster takes sonic centre stage with some prominent short phrases over Rossi and Parfitt's relentless rhythms, and Coghlan's powerhouse drumming.

Fast, urgent, and compelling, 'Is There A Better Way' is a brilliant display of what the band are capable of, and what the album as a whole has in store for the listener. It's stunning stuff.

'Mad About The Boy' (Rossi/Young) Duration: 3.32 Chord Count: 13

Fans could tell this was a Rossi/Young composition without having to check the sleeve. After the opener's intensity, 'Mad About The Boy' has the feel of a remake of 'Break the Rules' about it. We have the same foot-tappingly jaunty beat, plenty of piano in the mix, and Rossi's strong vocal melody, all contributing to a sense of familiarity.

There is, however, more to 'Mad About The Boy' than its distant cousin. Harmonically more complex and with a greater opportunity for Rossi to display his fretboard prowess, the song grooves along satisfactorily without dynamic or textural alteration. It's a good time boogie number that sounds like it's settling into a standard twelve-bar three chord formation for its duration. Then, at 1.03, the song modulates from B major to G sharp major for the bridge section, 'Don't tell me your troubles, I've got troubles that will make you scream and shout'. It transitions smoothly back into B major for the first guitar solo, which isn't far enough forward in the mix to be distinctive.

At 1.58, there is a repeat of the 'Don't tell me your troubles' section which moves into a repeat of the first verse. The brief introduction is reprised with some nifty rising arpeggio work from Parfitt into Rossi's final solo. The song concludes with a typical blues turnaround chord progression and a live ending.

'Ring Of A Change' (Rossi/Young) Duration: 4.14 Chord Count: 12

Mein Gott, how fast? Playing along to this without chemical enhancement is a bit of a test; I might have to get myself another cup of coffee.

'Ring Of A Change' is another 100-metre race of a song and is up there with 'Mean Girl', 'Is There A Better Way', and 'Rolling Home' as some of the quickest tracks the band would ever record. The introduction has 'Blue Eyed Lady' levels of complexity about it, comprising three distinct, very short sections; the first moves between C and G major with a low register rising bluesy melody, the second is rapid-fire chord work with vicious stabs from Coghlan, and the third is a higher-pitched, celebratory sounding chord sequence which descends chromatically until the song actually starts. And that's just in the first 30 seconds.

A high energy straight boogie rhythm kicks the main part of the track off with Rossi's high-pitched vocals soaring over the constantly driving rhythm section. The chorus, 'Move into the light … I'll see you in the light, alright', benefits from superior sounding backing vocals. The first part of the introduction is repeated leading into the second verse, which is quickly followed by another reprise of the first part of the introduction.

At 2.09, where the seasoned listener might be expecting a flurry of soloing, the song takes a sharp left turn and introduces a new chord sequence which is played three times. There is a short flourish of lead guitar before parts two and three of the introduction appear again. The third verse and chorus, both harmonised, then speeds on by. The first part of the introduction is played a final time, the chords climb back up to the tonic key, and Rossi's fade-out solo takes the vocal melody, and twists it round and round in the upper reaches of the fretboard.

'Ring Of A Change' is another stunner, too good to be a mid-side album track, and yet it's surrounded by some of the best writing and performances the band would ever produce. Never a live favourite or an A-side single release, this song is just too strong to be ignored in favour of more famous and, in some cases, less impressive tracks.

'Blue For You' (Lancaster) Duration: 4.04 Chord Count: 11

'Blue For You' is one of Lancaster's uncharacteristically introverted tracks and, as the album's only ballad, it's a strange choice as a title track. Which came first? The overtures from Levi Strauss which led to the song, or the song becoming the inspiration for an advertising campaign? Enquiring minds might be interested.

The track is a beautiful medium-slow blues filled with downbeat feeling. Restraint and control are the musical orders of the day here. Rossi excels with his lead fills and biting solo, the bassist's soft-toned vocals suit the melancholy lyrics, and elsewhere there are effective backing harmonies, and a subtle, persistent rhythm guitar accompaniment. Coghlan's drum patterns move the song along, preventing it from falling into the clichés of the genre.

There's a solid groove underneath the bridge section; 'Cheating and lying, I played around, living and dying you stood your ground', and the harmony vocals build into Rossi's solo, which is amongst the most expressive and effective of his work on the band's slower material. There are occasional flurries of notes, plenty of phrasing and feel, and real control in the emotions he wrings out of the guitar, especially in the latter half of his allotted sixteen bars.

The smooth harmonies and well-arranged instrumentation maintain the class through to the song's reflective end, with Rossi again underplaying his hand(s) to great effect.

'Rain' (Parfitt) Duration: 4.34 Chord Count: 5

Ah, Mr Parfitt. Welcome back; we've missed you!

Opening with a thunderous riff and an anvil-heavy rhythm that just refuses to let up, 'Rain' is a spectacular chunk of boogie metal that has style and power by the bucket-load. Parfitt is in fine voice, Lancaster throbs away at the bottom end magnificently, and Coghlan holds down the solid groove with a vice-like grip. At 1.20, a new chord progression backed by the ever-effective choral backing vocals is unleashed before a fantastic descending Parfitt riff is played four times over the relentless bass pedal A note. Rossi joins in an octave higher on the final time before his Chuck Berry-esque solo, which becomes more melodic in its second half.

At 2.31, the song moves into a bridge section; 'Now I can live without the rain that's falling on my head', before the riff returns for the third and final verse and chorus. A reprise of the choral chord section, with an increasingly busy Lancaster, bulldozes the song into its coda section, which fades away, again with the superior sounding backing vocal harmonies. 'Rain' was the first chart hit to feature Parfitt on vocals. For fans accustomed to Rossi's distinctive singing style, this was a departure and showed the depth of talent within the band.

'Rolling Home' (Lancaster/Rossi) Duration: 3.01 Chord Count: 8

This is a fabulous slice of countrified rock with a wonderful groove and clever interplay between the guitars. Based around a high energy riff, 'Rolling Home' is much more powerful and persuasive than 'Fine Fine Fine'. Bob Young's harmonica sounds superb here, providing plenty of atmospheric fills, and Lancaster tones his voice down a notch from its usual rock gruffness. At 0.42, there is a fabulous rising guitar riff underpinned by the pedal bass drive, which is repeated after each vocal section.

At 1.23, the instrumental section explodes with repeated rising power chords before subsiding into a harmonised, highly melodic guitar section that has echoes of Wishbone Ash to it. A simple chromatic melody is harmonised, and then harmonised again before the song kicks back in at 2.15 for the final verse and chorus. The track comes to an *uber*-tight ending with a classic blues turnaround sequence as Coghlan throws in a neat cymbal crash on the final up-beat.

'That's A Fact' (Rossi/Young) Duration: 4.19 Chord Count: 7

The band's critics should send their ears this way. 'That's A Fact' breaks new ground whilst remaining a powerful, grooving track. Underpinned by a relentless and yet counter-intuitively laid back two-in-the bar funk feel, it features Rossi on lead vocals with impressive backing harmonies on the refrain, 'And I'm alone, and that's a fact'. Coghlan is particularly impressive throughout, holding down the steady funk groove whilst keeping everything he plays interesting.

At 1.19, the music moves key into a bridge section with a new riff as its backbone, and at 1.28, there is a single bar of 3/8 time thrown in at the end of the six-bar phrase. This is a clever moment that is not repeated later in the section; it's just thrown in as a brief flurry of musical sleight of hand, which doesn't spoil the feel of the song one iota.

After the third verse, the song moves into an instrumental section which, like 'Rolling Home' before it, is carefully structured rather than just an opportunity for a display of fretboard fireworks. Commencing with a new, repeated chord progression, the track shows off its funk credentials even more between 2.31 and 3.03, where an excellent display of tight-yet-loose two bar funk phrases are played six times. The phrase mutates on the seventh time, leading back into the familiar groove, a repeat of the third verse, and the refrain appearing three times as a long fade sets in.

'That's A Fact' is both new and accomplished for a band brimming with confidence and ideas at this stage of their career.

'Ease Your Mind' (Lancaster) Duration: 3.12 Chord Count: 8

And the mood changes yet again, although the key of C major is maintained from 'Rolling Home' and 'That's A Fact'. Normally this type of repetition would lead to aural boredom (yes, AC/DC, I *am* thinking of you), but Lancaster's second contribution, another 'light-touch' affair, adds to the variety of styles on offer.

'Ease Your Mind' is a more traditional Quo number that drives along, but with a relaxed shuffle feel, it follows a conventional pattern of three vocal sections with an instrumental section before the third verse. The bassist's vocals are another example of the gentler side of his rocky nature, whilst Bown's honky-tonk piano adds much to the texture. Rossi plays an appropriately melodic solo over the vocal chord progression, and the song comes to an unusual close with a single person clapping and Lancaster murmuring 'Well, ladies and gentlemen, welcome to the Chris Lade ball', or perhaps it's '...welcome to the crystal lade bomb'. No, I don't know what it means either.

If *Blue For You* has a disposable song, 'Ease Your Mind' is it. Whilst it's an enjoyable enough three minutes, there is a lack of textural or dynamic alteration and, without a bridge section, or different musical interlude, attention is not stimulated. It's by no means a *bad* song, they would come next year, but it lacks the energy, bite, and creativity of the earlier tracks. Not to worry, though, here's Rick Parfitt to save the day with his closing contribution...

'Mystery Song' (Parfitt) Duration: 6.40 Chord Count: 6

'Mystery Song' is, with the possible exception of 'Breaking Away' from 1979's *Whatever You Want*, the band's last hurrah at an album-closing epic before cloying commerciality began to take hold. Whilst 'Mystery Song' doesn't have the structured complexity of 'Slow Train' or the improvisational genius of the latter half of 'Forty Five Hundred Times', what it does have (melody, power, and commitment), it has in spades. Parfitt composed the track whilst alone in the studio one night, having drunk a cup of tea to which Rossi had added a substantial quantity of speed. When the band returned the next morning, he was still there, still playing, and 'Mystery Song' was basically finished. Not a bad night's work, on reflection...

This is a song in three parts, or it's three separate songs strung together; take your pick. The first (0.00-1.13) is a dreamy introduction. Rossi and Parfitt's guitars chime off each other, Coghlan provides decorative ride cymbals and rim shots, and Lancaster has some beautiful melodic phrases weaving in and out of the soundscape. Parfitt's soft vocals are completely at odds with what is to come, as he sings over his modulated guitar effect ('I see that look on your face...') before the opening instrumental section is repeated.

At 1.14 the song proper starts, with a repeated descending major key chord sequence under which the band just explodes at 1.39. Then we are off to the races with Parfitt's tale of a rendezvous with a lady who requires coin-of-the-realm in exchange for the temporary pleasure of her company. The sound is titanic, a fantastic driving riff, pounding bass and drums, and intense vocals all adding to the overwhelming effect.

At 3.34, Rossi has an energetic solo and, at 3.59, a favourite musical trick of mine is performed as the rest of the band drop out, leaving just Parfitt riffing away. The break is only temporary as the band power back in a few seconds later for the third verse. The same device was used in 'Rain' (3.01) and 'Rolling Home' (3.36), and it's highly effective, allowing a brief respite whilst keeping the excitement level high before hitting the dynamic throttle hard again.

Finally, at 5.08, the number collapses, spent after its exertions, into a reprise of the opening ambient atmosphere. There are no more vocals; the music gathers power and at 6.04 lifts again, this time into a bemusing mix of funk and country (Funktry? Cunk?), and off into the distance it rides to a fade. When 'Mystery Song' was released as a single, it was only the powerful four-minute main section of the song which made it onto vinyl, the opening and closing sections were dispensed with. Why is it called 'Mystery Song'? I don't know; it's a mystery. Sorry.

Non-Album Track

'You Lost The Love' (Rossi/Young) Duration: 2.59 Chord Count: 4

The B side to 'Rain' is a lightly powered, commercial number that has catchy melodies in the verse and chorus, and a constant driving beat, but very little else to distinguish it. Opening with a pleasant country-esque descending guitar phrase, the song soon settles into its comfortable slippers for the musical equivalent of a nice sit down with a cup of tea and a chocolate biscuit. There are some good vocal harmonies and a tight, chunky little riff at the end of the chorus, but it follows a verse/chorus/repeat structure *ad nauseam*. Without a new section or any instrumental or dynamic variation, it tends to pass the ears by, leaving you wondering what's just happened. If anything.

'Wild Side Of Life' (Carter/Warren) Duration: 3.16 Chord Count: 5

Originally inflicted upon the world by Hank Thompson in 1952, 'Wild Side Of Life' became, for reasons which elude me, a massive hit. It is a beyond-parody traditional country song, riddled with slide guitars, a 'slow-bordering-on-lobotomised' tempo, scraping fiddles, and a mournful sounding, possibly concussed, vocalist. I've listened to it, so you don't have to. Quo's version, to be fair, at least rocked things up substantially.

This 'single only' release was produced by a friend of the band, Roger Glover, who also played bass as Alan Lancaster was in Australia with his family. It was the chart success of this song (released to support *Live!*, which, strangely, didn't emerge for a further three months) that inspired the band to seek an outside producer for their next album.

'Wild Side Of Life' is, frankly, dull. On the plus side, the introduction could have led somewhere interesting, Coghlan's bass drum gets some punishment, and Rossi's voice is ideally suited to the country rock genre, but once the plodding rhythm kicks in at 0.28, it's a long, slow slide down into monotony. Bown hammers away at his piano with energy, and the whole mix becomes heavier at 1.09, but the enterprise quickly becomes repetitive. There is a simple, melodic guitar solo, but it does nothing to lift matters. On and on it goes with nothing new or interesting happening, and eventually, it fades away.

The 2015 reissue of *Blue For You* included the demo version of the track, which is a *much* better listening experience. There's an intriguing slide country guitar sound slipped into the mix, plenty of cowbell, a more interesting blend of instruments, and the vocals have a rougher hue. There is also a better guitar solo. This version is in B major, a semitone above the official release, and whilst the song remains the same, the mix and arrangement are more raucous and involving.

'All Through The Night' (Rossi/Lancaster) Duration: 3.14 Chord Count: 6

The B-side to 'Wild Side Of Life' is a *much* better track and should really have displaced 'Ease Your Mind' on *Blue For You* to keep the second side's energy level up.

'All Through The Night' is really two songs, one Rossi's and one Lancaster's, glued together. Kicking off with a vigorous chord sequence, a bass-heavy rhythm leads into the chorus and verse, where yet again impressive backing vocals add class. The vocals are harmonised, and Bown is heard far back in the mix hammering away for all he's worth.

At 1.45, the new song comes in with a crunching riff and heavyweight syncopated drumming. Lancaster's rock voice, over-treated with reverb, is back over this high energy, but too brief, interlude. The 'drop-out' trick is played again, this time between 2.38 and 2.43 underneath the chorus vocals. Once the driving rhythm section is back in their seats, the song goes into a fade on repeated choruses.

'Getting Better' (Lennon/McCartney) Duration: 2.22 Chord Count: 5

All This And World War Two (catchy title, disastrous film) was a 1976 musical documentary made by 20th Century Fox in which footage from the Second World War was supported by 'modern day' artists covering the music of The Beatles. Stop shaking your heads at the back! *Somebody* thought it was a good idea...

Quo's allocated song is from *Sergeant Pepper's Lonely Hearts Club Band*. The original track lends itself to Quo's signature style, with its steady rhythm and highly melodic vocal line, which makes their interpretation all the more, let's be gracious, 'surprising'. No, let's not. Let's be honest. It's dire. The 'arrangement' features just Rossi on vocals, some grinding guitar in the background, and the, erm, London Symphony Orchestra. Of course.

If that wasn't bad enough, there is a bizarrely psychedelic and, simultaneously, 'Christmassy' feel to the arrangement. Ironically, 'Getting Better'... doesn't, and ends up being another entrant in the 'I've Listened So You Don't Have To' category.

Rocking All Over The World

Personnel:
Francis Rossi
Richard Parfitt
Alan Lancaster
John Coghlan
Guest musicians:
Andy Bown: piano
Frank Ricotti: percussion
Producer: Pip Williams
Engineer: John Eden
Mastered: Melvin Abrahams
Recorded at Studio Bohus, Kungalv, Sweden
Released on 26 November 1977
Highest chart position: 5
Weeks on chart: 15

By the middle of 1977, Status Quo had the majority of the rock music world at their feet. The band were huge, both in their homeland and across Europe, with an excellent back catalogue of significant album and single chart success, and had just released a successful double-live album, the 1970s badge of achievement.

One part of the globe, however, remained immune to their charms. America just hadn't taken to Quo, yet it wasn't for lack of trying on the band's part. They had toured the States several times but never managed to establish more than a foothold in the territory. For the first time in their career, and to avoid the punishing effects of the United Kingdom's taxation laws, the band decided to record overseas. It was hoped that a different location, and an outside producer, would produce the sort of polished results that meant even the United States would buckle under the Quo onslaught. Rossi was forthright about the decision, being quoted in the inlay booklet which accompanied the 2015 CD reissue;

The idea with *Rocking...* was to make an album that would be saleable to the American market. We lost fortunes going to the States but made money everywhere else, so it made good business sense. And it sold shit-loads, more than we normally did, but we received so many letters from fans saying 'Shoot the fucking producer'.

Lancaster's view was more succinct, also taken from the reissue CD booklet;

Back then, Quo was almost like a religion to the fans. To the band, it was like being in a football team; you were allowed to have the occasional bad game, but nobody wanted to hear us playing netball.

The bassist's sporting reference is interesting. Every Quo album since *Hello!* had featured some lighter pop-rock moments. Songs like 'Claudie' and 'Fine Fine Fine' were tolerated by the Quo Army as they didn't dominate the heavy soundscape. With the band's tenth studio outing, the needle swung dramatically to the lighter side of rock, and even touching the outright poppy side of the meter.

The netball referee chosen was Philip 'Pip' Williams. A talented musician, capable of playing several instruments, Williams was also an accomplished performer, composer, and arranger. The band felt that they were in danger of becoming predictable and wanted to broaden their sound and, hopefully, appeal still further. Vertigo wanted Williams to add some colour to the band's sound, and especially clean it up. Quo agreed with this assessment. However, in the CD booklet accompanying the 2015 reissue Williams confessed;

> With hindsight, I will agree that *Rocking...* would have been better with the sound pared down, but I was getting it in the neck from all sides. I will never forget Ken Maliphant, the boss at Vertigo, hearing the results at a playback and declaring, 'Have we got an album or what!?'

Well, yes, Ken, you *do* have an album. But it's the first and biggest in a series of musical missteps by the band.

Recording should have taken place in Dublin, but Williams found the chosen location to be technically unsuitable. Work had to be postponed again when John Coghlan suffered an acute case of appendicitis. It was the producer's decision to bring in session percussionist Frank Ricotti, who played a variety of tambourines, congas, and bongos on the album. Coghlan was relaxed about this, preferring just to play his drum kit.

The cover for *Rocking...* immediately set out the very different nature of the band's new stall. The familiar 'slanted-and-shaded' logo was replaced with a blue and white oscillating waveform design over a satellite image of the earth. The album title was printed in a dotted lettering moving horizontally along the bottom. The words 'Richter Scale 7.6' (a measurement of an earthquake's magnitude), and the album's catalogue number, '9102014', appeared in an overlaid red font. On the rear of the single sleeve was a live-action photo of the band. All three guitarists are facing Coghlan in what looks like an end-of-song power chord smash, below which the song titles were dotted across in the same red dot style used on the front. The 'From The Makers Of...' icons were displayed as coloured computer keys. For the time, it was a very modern-looking design, and emphasised a distinct break with Quo's immediate past.

The inner sleeve had a brown and white image of the Frantic Four on one side and a complex electronics diagram illustration on the other, with additional information appearing at various points in small print. The band's surnames only featured in the song writing acknowledgements, with the design being credited to Eric Howard productions. Overall, it looks desperate and downmarket compared to previous covers. Lancaster expounded his 'benefit-of-hindsight' view on the release in 'Status Quo – The Official 40th Anniversary Edition Biography';

> That was the beginning of the end. We'd produced ourselves up to that stage, and it was the biggest mistake every band makes, get somebody else in to work on the music that you're already successful in making. So in comes Pip Williams, and in come the strings, the chick singers, the brass, the keyboards, the triple tracked solos. What he did to us ruined us.

Williams is often viewed as the villain in this piece of Quo's history. However, in an interview for *Sound On Sound* in January 2009, he remained resolute about the record:

> I didn't stand there with a gun to their heads saying, 'Do this, it's going to be like this!' Everything was done with their approval when recording and producing that album.

The album and its famous title track single were *huge* successes, and the *Rocking*... tour was the band's biggest and most lucrative yet. Vast swathes of new fans joined the Quo Army. The long term fans, however, complained bitterly about the new sound. It seemed to them that Quo were selling their credibility in exchange for even greater wealth and fame, a case of integrity out, income in. This was an attitude that caused puzzlement within the band. Rossi explained in ...*X/S All Areas*;

> ...it was also the album that provoked the most complaints we've ever had, not merely from the critics this time, but from actual fans. In a nutshell, they accused us of going 'soft'. But we weren't thinking 'hard' or 'soft' when we were making the album, we were simply thinking 'good' or 'bad'. Up until then, that was always enough.

There was a premonition of this perceived softening in the band's sound; the previous year's standalone single 'Wild Side Of Life' had been nothing special and had signalled a more commercial approach to the charts. In a live situation, Quo continued to kick serious butt, but from this point on, the quality of the studio output was at best 'pretty good', and at worst 'very poor indeed'.

There are two things wrong with *Rocking*...; the songs and the sound. Apart from that, it's a fine album. Unusually it contained twelve tracks, leaving precious little room for the band's instrumental creativity. At least four of the tracks should have been drowned at birth. The remainder could, with either the band self-producing or with someone who knew how Quo should sound at the desk, have turned *Rocking*... into a half-decent offering. As it is, it's a *massive* disappointment. The introduction of outside writers for three of the numbers didn't help matters either.

And lurking in the background were the effects of years of near-constant touring and the never-ending pressure to improve on what had already been achieved. Personality issues were beginning to surface as a result of sustained drink and drug abuse and arguments regarding song writing royalties. It was a potent combination.

In 2015 *Rocking...* was reissued with an expanded version of the album, which was remixed by John Eden, who removed a lot of the aural clutter. In the CD reissue booklet he stated;

> I wanted to restore the original two guitars of Francis and Rick, plus bass and drums. I've stripped things down and kept everything as raw as possible; I even tweaked the occasional tempo. It took about four months and I think the results are amazing.

'Amazing' is be a bit of a stretch, given the rules regarding turd polishing, but the songs certainly *sound* a lot better. It's an interesting 'compare and contrast' exercise, and, unsurprisingly, the remix wins hands down every time. The disc also included demos of 'Dirty Water', 'Baby Boy', 'Hard Time', and 'Hold You Back', which are intriguing. 'Hold You Back', for example, doesn't feature the distinctive Celtic flavoured instrumental melody, whilst the others are fascinating snapshots of 'works-in-progress'.

'Hard Time' (Rossi/Parfitt) Duration: 4.44 Chord Count: 7

'Hard Time' opens with a nice throwback to the similar-sounding opening of 'Mystery Song' in its ambient introduction. There are some atmospheric arpeggios, gentle synthesizer washes (Erm, a *synthesizer*? On a *Quo* record?), and subtle cymbal swells over a gradually growing rhythm. Pounding drums kick off a chugging, mid-tempo, catchy riff 28 seconds in.

Rossi's vocals are set to maximum nasal for the verse, with backing voices joining in for the chorus, the texture being filled out with piano and plenty of percussion. The chorus refrain, 'So it's a hard time for us all till she gets it right' was apparently inspired by a family argument within the Rossi household.

Two verses and a chorus are followed by a further verse before an instrumental section (2.48-3.09). This features the riff, more percussion, and a belching synth in the lower end, but there is no guitar solo, or change in mood or feel. A repeated verse and two choruses finish the number off. If you can put up with the lightweight production, then things are off to a reasonably promising, if somewhat puzzling start.

'Hard Time' is a catchy song from the heavier end of the 'new era' Quo spectrum. The remixed version, although featuring more synthesizer, grooves better with more weight to the overall sound. But it's nobody's 'Is There A Better Way', 'Little Lady', 'Backwater', 'Roll Over Lay Down', or 'Don't Waste My Time'.

'Can't Give You More' (Rossi/Young) Duration: 4.15 Chord Count: 6

This is a fast-paced, driving pop-rocker with a similar template to 'Hard Time'. Once again, Rossi sings, there's an earworm of a verse and chorus melody with a relentless groove, and Bown hammers away at his piano for all he's worth. Here the emphasis is on commerciality, especially with the use of the relative minor chord in the chorus, but again there is very little, if any, variation in the instrumental texture.

Similarly, there is no bridge section, no solo, or even a separate instrumental section. The song rolls through a verse/chorus/repeat formula, which is a shame as with more creativity, it could have been much better. As it stands, 'Can't Give You More' ironically feels half-finished, and races off to a fade after what seems like a comparatively long time.

The remix version is much meatier, includes a count-in, and doesn't fade, whilst Coghlan and Lancaster make energetic contributions in the 'full' play-out section.

'Let's Ride' (Lancaster) Duration: 3.02 Chord Count: 6

What's too fast, finishes far too quickly, and disappoints throughout its duration? Eyebrows are quickly raised on hearing 'Let's Ride'. What, exactly, is going on here?

Inspired by Lancaster's newfound love of motorbikes, this is the first song on the album which just doesn't sound like Quo. At all. Looking for positives, it's an energetic, musically very busy song, which mixes funk and disco grooves over an aggressive rhythm section at a rapid tempo. Rossi has brief melodic solo moments, and there's an interesting instrumental section that features plenty of different ideas.

On the other, much more whelming, hand, this is a *very* average composition, especially lyrically. 'Let's Ride' sounds like it could be just about *any* rock band wanting to sound poppy and accessible. And it's about motorcycles.

The remix sounds heavier with a greater emphasis on the bass and Rossi's solos. The rhythm guitars are toned back, and the percussion is brought to the front of the mix, but it doesn't really matter how many knobs you twist, it isn't going to put a better finish on these shaky foundations.

'Baby Boy' (Rossi/Young) Duration: 3.09 Chord Count: 3

Make no mistake, 'Baby Boy' is awful. There's no other word for it. Actually, there are *a lot* of other words for it, none of which my editor would let me use.

With its tired tempo, light pseudo-reggae feel, and an unnecessary amount of synth in the mix, this is the album's nadir. And so soon! And that's a pretty low bar to get under. Bereft of any feature that could identify it as being a 'Quo' song, with the possible exception of Rossi's vocals, this track is as abysmal lyrically as it is insipid musically. We are treated, in the same way a patio is treated with weed-killer, to a journey through a man's life. Strap yourself in; this is going to hurt…

Initially, he is a little baby boy ('just to sit and play would be my joy'), then an older boy ('all the girls I wanted were my joy'), moving on to be an older lady's 'toy' (where 'thoughts of lust and wealth were now my joy'), and eventually reflecting on the life led. I am not making this up. Aspiring lyricists, welcome to 'Truly Terrible Song Writing 101'. 'Baby Boy' is a song to be avoided at all costs.

'You Don't Own Me' (Lancaster/Green) Duration: 3.02 Chord Count: 8

Lancaster wrote this unremarkable track with Mick Green, a former member of Johnny Kidd And The Pirates, and he later confessed to being unimpressed with it saying in the CD reissue booklet;

> Micky and I wrote some stuff together, but it wasn't a great partnership and 'You Don't Own Me' was the wrong style for Quo. We tried to make it a Quo song, but in my opinion, it didn't really work.

Not just your opinion, my friend. Starting with an underpowered guitar riff leading into a solid foot-stomping rhythm, 'You Don't Own Me' has a loose, funky feel to it that grinds away semi-satisfactorily. There's a more melodic section 44 seconds in, 'And now your snakeskin colours are flying, you're trying to hide your poison disguise, so wipe the crocodile tears that are falling, they only make me realise', which lifts the music with effective percussion. Beyond a mildly interesting section (1.13-1.21) where the riff twists with the inclusion of a minor second interval and a bridge section (1.50-2.04) which has some classy backing harmonies, there is nothing going on here which will excite the horses.

The remix is a little faster, a little heavier, and, with some decent lead guitar in the play-out, and is, therefore, a *little* better.

'Rockers Rollin'' (Parfitt/Lynton) Duration: 4.14 Chord Count: 4

'Rockers Rollin'' is the first and only song on the album that seems to have any real connection to *Blue For You*. Unfortunately, it comes across as a 'Parfitt-by-numbers' song, the singer stretching the limits of his vocal range, especially in the chorus. Written with former Savoy Brown singer Jackie Lynton, there's the very welcome return of plenty of energy and overdriven guitar amplifiers. Lyrically it's more than a tad desperate; 'Just let us ride, we don't wanna be tied, rolling our way back home, taking our time, only trucking a line, rolling our way back home, we're rockers rollin', yeah…'. It's a step, if not a very big or inspired one, in the right direction.

Again the remix presents a much better *sounding* song. Grinding guitars are at the forefront of the mix, the shimmering synth of the pre-chorus is further back in the soundscape, and Rossi's solo (almost submerged in the original version) is now clearly heard. It's adequate, but adequate isn't good enough.

'Rocking All Over The World' (Fogerty) Duration: 3.34 Chord Count: 4

John Fogerty, principal songwriter and front-man of Creedence Clearwater Revival, had released this song on his second solo album two years previously. It was Parfitt who persuaded Quo to cover it.

Fogerty's original has a driving rhythm and a similar tempo but differs strikingly from Quo's version with the singer's gritty, gruff vocal style and some very prominent country guitar fills. Interestingly the guitar solo is very close to that played by Parfitt (a rare lead outing for him), with the second solo featuring some honky-tonk piano. The instrumental 'drop out' chorus also features before the song fades away.

Quo's interpretation is so well known that comment seems superfluous. Bown's keyboard playing is a constant presence, Rossi adds the familiar simplistic, sing-a-long second solo, and the 'drop out' chorus is given greater emphasis with the addition of an F sharp diminished between the F and G major chords, which did not feature on the Fogerty release.

'Rocking All Over The World', backed with 'Ring Of A Change' was released as a single and reached number three in the charts. The writing was on the wall by this stage. Lancaster was living in Australia and refused to fly back to shoot a promotional video for the song, which led to Colin Johnson's idea of replacing him with a life-size marionette playing the bass. The video is available online and needs to be seen to be believed.

'Who Am I?' (Williams/Hutchins) Duration: 4.29 Chord Count: 11

The most 'classic Quo' sounding track on the album is not an inter-group composition. In the CD reissue booklet Williams explained

> That song began as a very slow shuffle. And let me be clear; it was on the album because Rick and Francis had both loved our demo and not due to me being pushy with the band. The band, as one, was up for doing it because it had a demanding chord structure.

Underpinned by a relentless groove, a delay pedal, and a sinewy bluesy riff in G major, 'Who Am I?' is the song which best combines the familiar Quo with their newfound desire to sell lots of records in America. I'm sorry, I meant to type 'add variety and exciting new sounds to their established style'. The use of pedal bass notes over which suspended and standard major chords hang is extremely effective. There are some wonderful interweaving guitar lines, and the vocal and chorus melodies, backed with impressive, multi-layered, vocal harmonies are strong.

Opening with just two guitars, bass is added for the verse and chorus, with organ and harmony vocals adding to the weight of the chorus. Drums join the party at 1.14. After the second chorus, there is an instrumental with understated guitar arpeggios dancing around the soundscape, before the song lifts with the bridge section, 'Am I the chain that keeps you from falling? Am I the thoughts going round in your head? Am I the night-time? Am I the morning? Am I a fool that you wish for dead?' Here the song modulates into C major and a full-blooded and emotive solo. The music stays in this key, the chorus sounding anthemic, and the music fades out with the instruments feeding off each other.

The remix has a greater separation and clarity between the guitars and is taken at a slightly quicker tempo. This is much more like it. And then, seemingly inevitably…

'Too Far Gone' (Lancaster) Duration: 3.08 Chord Count: 5
In the CD reissue booklet Lancaster said of his own composition:

> 'I'd put that one into the same bag as 'Let's Ride'; it could've been better. To me, it's in that 'average' bracket; it could've been taken further'.

Yes, indeed. It could have been taken outside and shot.

Wrong-footing the listener with a nine bar introduction, this anxious sounding fast track has too much synth and general musical busy 'stuff' going on. There's a commercial chorus, some squawking guitars, and a vaguely melodic bridge section, but, all-in-all, this is a song that fans should not have had to listen to. On the plus side, 'Too Far Gone' doesn't last long, but nor does standing barefoot on an upturned plug, although the effects are similar. The song comes to a tight end, crashing almost immediately into…

'For You' (Parfitt) Duration: 2.59 Chord Count: 9
This is an island of saccharine blandness in an ocean of mediocrity. Parfitt's love song to his then-wife features dreamy sounding vocals, plenty of acoustic guitars, a relaxed tempo, and a tranquil, holiday-like feel.

The problem is this song lacks the structure and integrity of the band's earlier and better ballads and soon becomes another wearisome diversion for the ears. The sound is mushy, and the overall mood is cloyingly sweet. It's musical candyfloss, rather than pointedly romantic. On the very limited plus side, Rossi has a pleasingly melodic solo. It really shouldn't be the high point of the song. Nevertheless, it is. Next.

'Dirty Water' (Rossi/Young) Duration: 3.48 Chord Count: 6
In the CD reissue booklet Bob Young admitted;

> Yeah, Francis and I are big fans of country music. Quite a few of our songs began life in that vein. It wasn't even written specifically as a Quo song but it just seemed to work.

For those fans feeling disappointed by the lack of country rock on the album, worry not; your time has come. 'Dirty Water' is your archetypal Rossi/Young composition; simple in structure, strongly melodic, and almost irresistibly catchy. It would prove to be a great crowd sing-a-long at gigs and is as lightweight as it is irresistible.

After an all band introduction, Rossi sings the chorus over a solitary strummed guitar. The arrangement grows with percussion, bass, guitar fills and sustained organ, and, by the time we get to the tuneful solo, the song is in full swing. 'Dirty Water' has a certain 'Gerdundula'-esque charm to it, and it passes a few minutes by in a cheerful enough fashion, but in terms of an impressive album track, it, like so many of its bedfellows, is found significantly wanting.

'Hold You Back' (Rossi/Young/Parfitt) Duration: 4.25 Chord Count: 8
It's been a long wait, but finally, Quo unleash a decent song for the album closer. The opening Celtic style melody was Parfitt's contribution to the track, and it kicks 'Hold You Back' into a classic groove, as some harmonised guitars feedback tastefully into the Rossi-led verse.

Vocal harmonies join in for the highly addictive chorus and stay for the second verse. After the second chorus, we have the Celtic tune twice, once in D major then falling down into the introductory key of A major, before another verse and chorus. The Parfitt melody is so good it makes another appearance in the keys of D and A, before returning to D as the song enters its final straight, with a new and different guitar melody fading away over the relentless rhythm.

'Hold You Back' would become a live favourite, and rightly so. Sadly much of the rest of the album is forgettable, and although the title track would lift the band commercially into another league, this collection left fans wondering whether the band's best song writing and recording days were behind them.

And that's *Rocking*… for you. Four good songs and an acceptable cover version out of twelve tracks, it's either a brave experiment or an abject failure. It's certainly not a good ratio. Musically diverse, sonically and emotionally uninvolving, it left fans feeling confused, disappointed, saddened, or apoplectic depending upon their degree of devotion to the band. It could only be hoped that, having got this out of their system, their next offering would show a return to form.

If You Can't Stand The Heat...

Personnel:

Francis Rossi

Richard Parfitt

Alan Lancaster

John Coghlan

Guest musicians:

Andy Bown: keyboards

Frank Ricotti: percussion

Jacquie Sullivan, Stevie Lange, Joy Yates: additional vocals

The David Katz Horns: brass instruments

Bud Revo: horns

Producer: Pip Williams

Engineer: John Eden

Assistant Engineer: Freek Feenstra

Mastered by Melvyn Abrahams at Strawberry Mastering, London

Recorded at Wisseloord Studios, Hilversum, Netherlands

Released on 11 November 1978

Highest chart position: 3

Weeks on chart: 14

Quo's financial success meant that, for taxation purposes, the band had to live abroad for a twelve-month period; Lancaster went to Australia, Coghlan decamped to the Isle of Man, Parfitt moved to Jersey, whilst Rossi transferred to Eire. This geographical separation did nothing for band unity. Another financial effect was that their next album could not be recorded in the United Kingdom.

By now, drug and alcohol abuse was running rampant within the band, relationships were breaking down, and marriages were breaking up. The cracks were beginning to show, a result of a decade of almost non-stop touring, performing, writing, and recording, and no amount of substances, legal or illegal, could affect the necessary repair. A seismic shift in one of the band's best performing song writing teams was also on the horizon.

A financial advisor at Quarry saw the state Quo was in for most of the time and began to take advantage of them. The band was unaware of his activities, but Bob Young, an efficient tour manager, could tell something was significantly wrong. Chinese whispers soon became hard arguments and, by 1980, Young would have no more input into the Quo machine. His writing partnership with Rossi also came to an end as the guitarist moved on to another lyricist, Bernie Frost.

The theme of the cover for *Rocking...* had been to equate the band's sound to that of an earthquake. In reality, it had felt more like a minor tremor. Did the earth move for you? No, not really. With ...*Heat*... the visual focus was on temperature. The clever front cover image of a vinyl record as an electric spiral cooking hob complete with a hovering record needle was by the design company Hothouse. The gatefold sleeve, by 'Shoot That Tiger', resembled a gigantic book of matches which, when opened from the bottom, not the usual side, had a silhouette of Coghlan behind his drums, surrounded by stage smoke. The rear of the cover had a shot of Parfitt, Rossi and Lancaster live on stage, with Coghlan and his kit only just visible. The comparison with the sterile, precise feel of *Rocking...* was marked. The return of the 'slanted and shaded' band logo (also showing the effects of exposure to heat from underneath) was clearly intended to show that Quo were 'back', and the sound was 'hot'.

The visuals looked promising. There was both hope and expectation amongst the established fan base that 'normal service' would now be resumed. Even the new album's title, a truncation of the famous phrase attributed to the 33rd President of the United States, Harry S Truman; ('If you can't stand the heat, get out of the kitchen'), suggested that this could be a return to the high watermark of *Blue For You.*

The rear sleeve proudly proclaimed that the Aphex Aural Exciter had been used in the record's production. This electronic device manipulated and enhanced certain aspects of an instrument's signal to make the recorded sound more 'alive' for the listener. Would this be the case? Possibly. However, further investigation of the sleeve revealed a potential problem.

The retention of the much-maligned Pip Williams as producer suggested that the band still had their heart set on cracking the United States. At the time, Parfitt, banging the promotional drum, said;

> I think it is one of the best albums that we've made. Pip Williams must take some of the credit as he's pulled a lot of things out of the band.

Clearly, hype springs eternal. One of the 'things' Williams has managed to pull out of the band is, apparently, the ability to write really good songs. With *...Heat...* there's a continuing commerciality allied to a tendency to throw new instrumentation into the mix, just for the sake of it. In addition, we are treated to three female backing vocalists. Okay, but why? The answer is America. Williams defended himself, yet again, this time in the inlay booklet which accompanied the 2016 CD reissue;

> If anybody had a problem with the girl singers, then nobody voiced it to me at the time. In fact, Rick Parfitt had heard some other things I was working on outside of Quo, and he rather liked the idea of bringing them on board for a few tracks. It really was a case of adding a few other colours and the band were well up for that.

Okay, but a horn section. A *horn* section? On a *Status Quo* record? Why? The answer, again, is America. This album had better be good... but it isn't. And that's not just my opinion: Lancaster talked about the recording process in the 2016 CD reissue booklet:

The strange thing is that I actually welcomed Pip (to the project). I remember thinking 'This is how all the big spenders do it'. But then reality dawned. When you spend a week getting a bass drum sound, everyone gets bored. We'd never worked like that before. The spark ends up dying and the groove and the syncopation become lost. To me, it was bullshit. Talk of America was going on in the background, and we were being shaped into something we're not. The bottom line was that Pip Williams changed the sound of Status Quo.

...Heat... is, fundamentally, a pop-rock album, with some vague flashbacks to a heavier past. Both sides of the vinyl release were book-ended with reasonable rockers, but the rest of the album contained some of the most life-sapping, infuriating, and stodgy sounding material this line-up of the band would produce. There are lots of sonic production 'bells and whistles' to marvel at, if that's your thing, but, yet again, it's the songs that let the side(s) down. The overall recorded *sound* is preferable to that of *Rocking...*, but that isn't a difficult achievement. How much of the credit for this improvement should be given to the Aphex Aural Exciter isn't clear, but what is obvious is that the band needed better material, and a much harder rocking production. Parfitt, wearing his twenty-twenty hindsight glasses, attested to this in 1993:

I think we were starting to get a bit too clever. We'd been smoothed out, the rawness was gone. It could have been a great record, but the drums were awful.

Fair point, but *good songs* are the backbone to any album. And six of the ten tracks on *...Heat...* involved writers from outside the 'Quo-Zone'. Jackie Lynton, Mick Green, and now Bernie Frost appeared as co-composers. Andy Bown was involved with three numbers, and the Williams/Hutchins partnership returned, this time with the car crash that is 'Accident Prone'.

'Again And Again' (Parfitt/Bown/Lynton) Duration: 3.38 Chord Count: 10

The first single from the album, 'Again And Again' was released on 25 August 1978 (with, inexplicably, the dull-a-thon which is 'Too Far Gone' as its B-side) reaching number thirteen during its nine-week run on the charts.

Getting the obvious jibe out of the way first, yes, the word 'again' appears 64 times in the song. Glad to have cleared that up. Of more interest are Parfitt's mumbled words over the introduction. He could be saying 'Sing along, keep the album loose', or it might be 'Sing along, kick out the blues'. Or perhaps he's suffering a bout of self-awareness; 'Remember when we used to be good?'.

The new 'Williams Effect' is heard immediately. Sustained notes from the brass section sit over the opening power-chord section, then the music moves into a 'half-time' rhythmic groove, with plenty of busy percussion in the mix. Parfitt delivers a typical barky rocker from the upper end of his vocal range, the lyrics loosely covering the early history of rock'n'roll. The chorus canters away in double time before lapsing back for the second verse. After the next chorus, there's a typically melodic Rossi solo (2.03-2.29), with some powerful chord syncopations at its conclusion. Then, predictably, we are into a third verse, repeated choruses, and a tight live ending.

Energetic, noisy, and good fun, 'Again And Again' is a decent album opener without being classy enough to reach 'classic' status. On the plus side, the band sound is lively and engaging, there's plenty going on, and the chorus, whilst being aural cat-nip for the critics, is catchy and involving. On the minus side, you now have to endure, not enjoy, three more tracks before another good song comes along...

'I'm Giving Up My Worrying' (Rossi/Frost) Duration: 3.00 Chord Count: 7

Bernie Frost first made a writing appearance with 'A Year' on *Piledriver*, which he co-wrote with Lancaster. Here he and Rossi cook up a fluffy little commercial number with plenty of guitars, a head-nodding tempo, and a rhythmic reliance on Coghlan's bass drum on the fourth beat of the verse bars. There are vocal harmonies, lots of percussion, and a general feel of positivity in this major key poppy rocker, but crucially it is also *massively* banal. The song seems more suited to a country music album (albeit with different instrumentation) or the type of 'message' tune to be adopted as an anthem at a children's camp to reinforce self-esteem.

There's a brief half-time feel, melodic instrumental interlude (1.09-1.17), which is repeated (2.15-2.22), and the song begins to bore itself into a fade with a heavy bass drum beat, agitated percussion, and Rossi's between-lyrics fills. There are too many cooks in this particular kitchen and not enough good ingredients. It's only the second song and already I'm thinking of leaving...

'Gonna Teach You To Love Me' (Lancaster/Green) Duration: 3.09 Chord Count: 9

And the mind isn't changed by this oddity. What starts out as a typically commercial, post *'Blue For You'* Quo track (a rolling rhythm, easily anticipated chord progressions, and Lancaster's rock vocals), is spoilt by the added instrumentation (a chorus effect on the mid-range guitar melody, more frantic percussion, and some desperately cheesy organ tones). This just isn't good enough.

The song takes a truly bizarre turn after the second verse into a bridge section (0.57-1.24) which could have been lifted from any number of 1960s pop love songs. Added into the mix are some high pitched, harmonised background vocals and what sounds like a steal from the chorus of 'Ice In The Sun' (where a plectrum was strummed across piano strings to add a zingy effect to the music).

Then, in a bizarre 'nothing to see here, move along please' kind of way, there's the third verse. This leads into Rossi's solo, with Coghlan seemingly relishing the opportunity to give his drums some serious punishment. As the song hits its final fading stretch, the mix gets even busier with still heavier drums, backing vocals, more cheese on the organ, and a revolving lead guitar melody. In the 2016 CD reissue booklet Lancaster said of the track:

> I still like the song, but I really wish it had had a bit more grunt behind it. To me, the way it was recorded didn't sound natural enough.

All those in agreement, raise your hands…

'Someone Show Me Home' (Rossi/Frost) Duration: 3.51 Chord Count: 11

Oh dear God. Taxi!

If you thought 'Baby Boy' was the worst song the band had committed to vinyl since the late 1960's, think again. 'Someone Show Me Home' is desperately poor. No, it's worse than that, it's dire and a marker for the sort of shoddy goods the band would regurgitate on a regular basis when Rossi and Parfitt revived the name in the mid-1980s. This song is the musical equivalent of finding a used Band Aid in a limp salad.

Time to get off the fence, I guess. 'Someone Show Me Home' is a slow, waltz where, for once, the lyrics are better than the music, 'Down by the side of the hotel all-nighter is your old grey door, men gather round with the fear that a lawman will come to clean up the floor, once a week it all begins, 10.15 for sure.' These are evocative lines, inspired by scenes Rossi had witnessed when staying in an Amsterdam hotel one night.

Musically, however, it's a ghastly, sickly sweet morass of Hammond organ, acoustic guitar, and backing vocals, all stirred together with a sludgy tempo and topped off with an overwhelming sense of lethargy. Rossi is singing at the absolute top of his vocal range, and plays a mournful guitar solo which dies away, leaving the organ once again dominating the sound into the fade.

Yes, we *have* all had a great time, yes, it *has* been a brilliant evening, and we've all had a few drinks, but now it's time to go home, Karen.

'Long Legged Linda' (Bown) Duration: 3.26 Chord Count: 12

Finally! A really good rock song. It feels like it's been a long time coming. Although credited to Parfitt and Bown on the sleeve, 'Long Legged Linda' was actually just Bown's work and was based on an encounter when his own band was touring America. And the US of A looms large, both musically and lyrically, 'Well if you're ever in Los Angeles, and you've got time to spare, take a stroll up Sunset Boulevard, you'll find The Whiskey there'.

But it's the instrument arrangement that takes the shine off this tremendous number. The song brims with energy and attitude, but there's just *too much* going on. Whether it's the substantial and unnecessary presence of the horn section, a near-constant manic tambourine part, too much honky-tonking piano, or the over-the-top female singers, the arrangement puts the listener in mind of Meat Loafs' 'Dead Ringer For Love'. A great song, to be sure, but not the sort of music Quo should be aping. It makes the band sound like musical tourists, covering themselves with American trappings, which detract from what is, so far, the best track on the album.

The introduction, which appears three more times, moves through three keys before settling into an up-tempo groover, with Parfitt giving full force to his vocals. The chorus is both powerful and commercial, with a two-bar breather where the music moves into half tempo under the words, 'Playing The Whiskey to-*night*', as the song moves back into the original speed.

At 1.54, the first part of the introduction is reprised before Rossi has a short solo. This leads into a repeat of the third verse, repeated choruses, and cruises to a tight end with another excerpt from the introduction.

In the same way that *Rocking...* benefited substantially from a recent remix, it would be interesting to hear 'Long Legged Linda', and the few other good numbers on this album ('Again And Again', 'Oh! What A Night', and 'Like A Good Girl') given a similar John Eden style 'stripped-back' treatment. If we could lose all the sonic decoration and capture the muscular rock vibe that underpins these tracks, then ...*Heat*... would have a lot more going for it.

'Oh! What A Night' (Parfitt/Bown) Duration: 3.42 Chord Count: 5

Recorded in drop D tuning (where the lowest pitch string of the guitar is flattened by a tone from the standard E to a low D), 'Oh! What A Night' has a delicious, low-slung groove running constantly through it. The opening guitar rhythm would be used to even better effect on the title track of the band's next album. Here the introduction's shuffle riff is swamped with some swirling synthesizers before a five-note descending minor melody leads into the first verse.

The celebratory major key feel of the song is at odds with the melancholy lyrics, 'Walking the tightrope and losing my pole, I hung on by my teeth, one of those nights that didn't feel too right, gonna cry myself to sleep'. The backing singers are straight in with the chorus, again adding way too much, way too soon.

The music modulates upwards three semitones for Rossi's jaunty solo, with plenty of organ playing in the background. There's a repeat of the introduction and then a third verse; 'I picture your face, I keep on hearing your voice, I'm dying in these sheets, I daren't think too much, so I drink too much, I still can't get to sleep' before the final chorus and the play-out fade section. Here the girls go for it in spectacular fashion, including, at 3.21, a moment where it sounds like one of them stubs her toe.

Again, another good rocker is spoilt by too much background busy-ness. Lose the keyboards, keep the girls away from the mics, and you're well on your way to something really worthwhile. Parfitt would revisit the song's simple but highly effective central groove next year. Lancaster was also paying attention, storing the riff away for future use on one of the last great songs this line-up would produce.

'Accident Prone' (Williams/Hutchins) Duration: 5.03 Chord Count: 7

So, we've had two decent back-to-back rock songs, albeit with some sonic misgivings. It must be about time to redress the balance. First up is this lousy, funked up, disco-lite, commercially overbearing pile of aural confusion.

A shortened version of 'Accident Prone', with almost a minute of excess fat cut off, and backed with the 'better-but-that's-not-saying-much' 'Let Me Fly', was released as the album's second single on 17 November 1978. It only got as far as number 36 and spent a mere eight weeks in the charts. It seemed as though the fans really didn't care too much for Quo's perverse new direction.

There's an awful lot wrong with 'Accident Prone'. Coghlan's cymbal rhythm is redolent of the pervasive disco obsession which dominated pop music during the latter half of the Seventies. Meanwhile, Lancaster has a suspiciously funky bass line, whilst the guitar rhythm is distinctly and annoyingly syncopated. The whole thing is over-processed with chorus effects and the synthesizers, making unwelcome intrusions at most given opportunities.

The opening guitar rhythm is a slightly faster 'reinterpretation', shall we say, of The Beatles' 'Get Back'. The rhythm section soon begins their monotonous backing as the song itself opens with its harmonised chorus. Then it's verse, chorus, verse, chorus, and so on. There are no dynamics or textural variation at any point beyond the instrumental section (2.26-3.05), which features a highly processed, 'squawky' lead guitar tone, which is pretty much the noise a duck makes when placed in a microwave on full power. Apparently.

This section is reprised in the play-out from 4.15 until the eventual fade some 45 tiresome seconds later. Worryingly Rossi sounds perfectly at home singing this, and it's tricky to see what the appeal of this track is, beyond its obvious trend-following hope of chart-topping success.

'Stones' (Lancaster) Duration: 3.53 Chord Count: 4

Another contender in a very wide field for the 'Most Disappointing Song On The Album' award, 'Stones' is very, very dull indeed. The introduction is the only interesting part. Over an arpeggiated guitar, a sustained melody on a synthesizer is harmonised over and over until a mid-tempo tub-thumping rhythm takes hold and, like a puppy with a bone, just won't let go. Bad dog. No biscuit.

The chorus has the female singers making a return, and a church organ sound joins for the second verse. The lyrics are more of the 'woe-is-me' default setting of uninspired rock, although again, the major key setting sends mixed messages, especially with the jolly, sing-a-long chorus. The music moves up a key for the brief instrumental solo, with Rossi's over-processed guitar sound sounding more cockerelly than rocky. Then, predictably, there's a third verse, repeated choruses, and an instrumental fade out.

'Stones' is just another weak, overtly commercial, busy sounding song that is exactly the sort of discarded musical offal on the abattoir floor the critics would, rightfully, lambast. It's flabby, uninvolving, and works only as another showcase for flashy production techniques rather than genuine rock inspiration. In the reissue booklet Williams reflected on the track:

'Rick and Francis hated that song and Spud (John Coghlan) agreed, so there was a lot of politics to overcome to make it work'.

If three-quarters of the band didn't like the song, then what the hell is it doing on the album?

Lancaster concurred in the CD booklet;

Yeah, 'Stones' began as a shuffle and we couldn't work out whether it should be more of a hard rock thing, so I ended up completely rewriting the whole thing. It's still not a great song, but it's not bad, I suppose.

Think again.

'Let Me Fly' (Rossi/Frost) Duration: 4.22 Chord Count: 6
'Let Me Fly' is reminiscent of 'Mad About The Boy' and 'Don't Waste My Time', but it manages to fall a long way short of their quality. It has got, however, all this album's signature traits running through it. The horn section is at it again, the percussionist is overly audible, there's too much piano in the mix, and the track is highly commercial with another bouncy groove to it. The chorus has some latent hum-ability, but, at its core, 'Let Me Fly' is just another attention-dodging song on an album overpopulated with such disappointments. It gives the impression the band are either tired, or bored, or both.

There's a short harmonised lead guitar section after the second chorus (where else?), and plenty of vocal harmonies are thrown in using the go-to production philosophy of 'Everything and the kitchen sink'. It all sounds so *laboured*. The instrumental section is reprised for the fading play out, where all the available instruments are filling every imaginable place in the sound spectrum. You can just picture the recording desk; every single channel merrily bouncing along with green LEDs, all filled with signal, all competing for space, and none of them being distinctive or interesting enough to warrant it.

'Like A Good Girl' (Rossi/Young) Duration: 3.24 Chord Count: 6
And after what has been a further three-song torpor, the goodies are finally served up once again. Leaving the best till last isn't always a good strategy, but at least this album goes out with a bang rather than a whimper.

'Like A Good Girl' is an up-tempo, good-natured, energetic romp of a song that manages to overcome the intrusions of the brass section and the seemingly omnipresent honky-tonk piano. Luckily, the backing singers have been given the day off. The chorus is melodic and catchy whilst retaining power and conviction. There's a fast-paced instrumental section that *really* kicks (1.46-2.06). Here, for once, Rossi shows he can play some proper lead guitar rather than some of the solos-by-numbers he has offered up in most of the earlier songs on this album.

A final verse and chorus lead into an effective fading play out where guitar melodies bounce from channel to channel, whilst the blowers continue to provide a constant pain from the brass. Strip them and the piano out of the mix, and you have Quo cruising joyfully in some form of a 'return-to-form' song. Does anyone have John Eden's e-mail address?

That still leaves ...*Heat*... with only four decent songs, and more filler than a renovated Volkswagen Camper Van. The fact that this album achieved a higher chart placing than *Rocking...* during its fourteen-week run is perplexing. Yes, it *sounds* better than its predecessor, but that's all it does. A year earlier Pip Williams had overseen a clinically clean, critical disappointment and with this offering the band had been sent sonically way-out-westward to very limited effect. At this stage of their career, Quo were drifting, musically, professionally, and personally. There was, luckily, time for one last loud 'Hurrah' where the band managed to pull the musical rabbit/penguin out of their collective hats...

Whatever You Want

Personnel:
Francis Rossi
Richard Parfitt
Alan Lancaster
John Coghlan
Guest musicians:
Andy Bown: keyboards
Bob Young: harmonica
Producer: Pip Williams
Mastered by Marquee Studios, London
Recorded at Wisseloord Studios, Hilversum, Netherlands
Released on 20 October 1979
Highest chart position: 3
Weeks on chart: 14

Despite the commercial success of ...*Heat*... both band and fans were disappointed with the record. A return to their core sound, one without clinical over-production or additional instrumentation, was urgently required. While this was a wise decision it made the retention of Pip Williams as producer all the more puzzling. With the band resolving to pay greater attention in the studio, it was hoped that this would be third time lucky. Prior to the record's release, Parfitt said;

> We have picked up on the criticisms from fans that our last two albums were over-produced, and the new album has a more raw sound and live feel.

Recorded began in Hilversum in December 1978, with the final mixing being carried out in London the following March. Fortunately, this time Williams managed to produce a more focused, and rocking album; *Whatever You Want* drives along with only a single ballad among the various boogie, blues rock, and pop-rocking compositions.

The original title, *As It Happens,* had to be discarded when the band Dr. Feelgood released a live album with the same name in May 1979. A further delay ensued when Phonogram required changes after hearing the original master tapes, meaning that the release date was put back to the autumn. To whet the appetite of the fans, the now-title track was released as a single in September 1979, reaching number four as part of its nine-week run in the charts.

The album cover, the first not to feature any image of the band whatsoever since *Ma Kelly...*, was intriguing. Continuing the trend initiated with *Quo*, Coghlan, Rossi, Parfitt, and Lancaster were only named on the rear of the sleeve, with no allocation of instruments or vocal duties. Designed by Design Machine, with the illustrations by Andrew Aloof, and Alan Schmidt, the single sleeve featured an interior view of an American hotel foyer, set sometime in the mid-1950s. A crowd of people are staring at the vinyl-holding viewer, including a saluting doorman, a female television reporter, and a young boy who is wearing a small green badge displaying the image of a penguin. Further back are some press photographers, journalists, a businessman in formal dinner attire, (a 'penguin' suit) and, bizarrely, a Marilyn Monroe look-a-like. The crowd, now consisting of general members of the public, stretches indistinctly into the distance, shielded by camera flashes. The familiar band logo was displayed in white with red shading, with the album title in a packing-case style blue font, both caught in the glare of a flashlight.

On the rear of the sleeve is the perplexing image of a penguin wearing a red suspender belt waddling on a roped off red carpet somewhere amidst the crowd of onlookers. What is going on here, exactly? Is the penguin the celebrity? Is the penguin something that the celebrity has requested? Is the penguin a sardonic commentary on the temporary and meaningless nature of celebrity? Is the front cover crowd actually looking at a penguin? Am *I* the penguin? It would explain a lot. Did I ever imagine typing the word 'penguin' in an album review eight times? This has started to get seriously out of flipper, sorry, hand.

Penguins aside (damn it, nine!) *Whatever You Want* is Quo's best album since *Blue For You*. The writing is more 'in-house' this time. Whilst Rossi and Frost provide three of the ten tracks, the contributions from Parfitt, Bown and Lancaster, whether composing singularly or in partnership, have a reassuring quality. That said, *Whatever You Want* isn't as good, or as varied, as any of the five 'Golden Era' (*Piledriver-Blue For You*) albums, but it is a determined and mostly successful attempt to regain the ground lost with the two previous Williams productions. There is more than a waft of inherent commerciality to some of the tracks, but this is generally kept submerged beneath some excellent rocking performances. The clean, poppy sterility of *Rocking...*, and the unnecessary instrumental indulgences of *...Heat...* are gone. What remains is a solidly guitar-centric collection with a tight production which wasn't, however, without it's surprises. The second single to be issued from the album, Parfitt's languid, acoustic-based ballad 'Living On An Island', completely wrong-footed the critics. Rossi made the following valid point in an interview with BBC Radio in November 1979;

> There was always this thing of 'the singles are all the same...', and as soon as we did 'Living On An Island', the first question was 'Why have you done something so different?' which is so frustrating as soon as you did something different. And yet when people look back, they still say they're all the same.

This conundrum notwithstanding, the song became another top five hit and served to broaden the band's appeal even further. Radio stations lapped it up, and millions of listeners began to realise perhaps that there was more to Quo than common preconceptions and the press made out. This greater commercial success served to widen the divide in the growing fan base. The long term 'hard-core' Quo Army were now being joined by an ever-increasing swathe of new fans, attracted as a result of the recent, more commercially aligned hits.

Fortunately, *Whatever You Want* succeeds because, despite the obvious pop potential of its two singles, they were not the entire story. It is closer to the bright sounding, powerful *On The Level* era Quo, albeit with a more polished, controlled, and, this time, well-produced sound. Despite the behind the scenes personal issues, the album has a cohesiveness to it, both in its sound and the welcome return to some degree of compositional form.

Pip Williams' involvement is much less obvious and Quo appeared to be returning to what they did best. There is a commercial appeal under some seriously rocking grooves, quality song writing, and a *joie de vivre* that has been largely absent since 1976.

'Whatever You Want' (Bown/Parfitt) Duration: 4.02 Chord Count: 14

The brief arpeggiated introduction, in 3/4 time, bears no relation to the song that follows, beyond being in the same key of D major. Parfitt utilises the 'dropped D' tuning to achieve greater bass and sustain to his chords.

There's a neat production touch as the shuffle rhythm begins 25 seconds in; the amount of reverb is gradually decreased as the riff is repeated. By the time the key shifts from minor to major (0.41,) the effect has disappeared, bringing a greater immediacy and attack to the famously addictive chord sequence which dominates the rest of the song.

'Whatever You Want' doesn't follow a conventional structure. The vocals start with a harmonised chorus at 1.12 before moving into the first verse, which Parfitt sings alone. The music moves then into the bridge section, 'I can take you home on the midnight train again, I could make an offer you can't refuse' before Rossi's spiky melodic solo. Thankfully his 'Microwaved Mallard' tone of ...*Heat*... is no more; he plays the 'not-as-easy-as-they-sound' phrases with a much better lead guitar sound. The harmonic structure of the instrumental section is also more complex than the repetitive nature of the rest of the song would suggest, with subtle modulations taking the music through a further three keys before arriving back at another verse. A repeated bridge and an altered chorus bring the song to a false stop, before the fading play out of the resolutely catchy riff.

In his autobiography Rossi admitted to some jealousy of the song, as well as providing an excellent summation of its long-term success:

I hadn't come up with anything that good since 'Down Down', five years before. Rick sings it brilliantly, too. Fair play, it's simply one of those songs that completely defines and reaffirms the Quo musical identity. It's also got that great quality all the best songs have of having universal appeal. It's suggested there in the title, of course, 'whatever you want, here it is – you can have it'. But it's in the glorious rhythm and riff too. Your body starts reacting to it before your brain even knows what's going on. Your feet tap. Your head nods. Your shoulders start to twitch. As a result, it was a major hit in every country it was released in ... and remains one of the big highlights of any Quo show to this day.

'Shady Lady' (Rossi/Young) Duration: 3.00 Chord Count: 9

Unlike *Rocking...* and *...Heat...* there is no second song slide into mediocrity with *Whatever You Want*. 'Shady Lady' is a rapid, major key rocker, full of driving rhythms and powerful hooks. Rossi's guitar has a strong melodic line leading into the first verse, with some typical rock and roll stylistic devices in the background of the chorus refrain. His solo is another brief, tuneful interlude on top of the relentlessly powerful rhythm section.

The play-out has some high-pitched backing vocals, which are less than effective. Bown is just about heard, keeping himself busy in the back of the mix, filling out the texture with some honky-tonk piano. 'Shady Lady' is fast, furious, and packed with energy; a statement of intent for the rest of the album.

'Who Asked You' (Lancaster) Duration: 3.57 Chord Count: 11

A Lancaster song with some lyrical bite, 'Who Asked You' is a song of defiance, giving the musical finger to the critics; 'There you go again telling me the same mistakes I made, there you go again, telling me the way I should have played'.

Opening with a bluesy, rolling lower string melody backed with sustained chords, the song suddenly picks up the power 21 seconds in as a classic Quo rhythm breaks forth. There's a yell of joy from someone as Coghlan's drum fill unleashes a mighty groove to great effect. Delivered at a medium tempo within a major key and underpinned by more solid rhythmic backing, the verse and chorus melodies remain highly melodic. The chorus lyrics are equally hard-edged; 'Who asked you to prey on my feelings, lying low in every cloud? Who asked you? I've never been the one to give you any kind of reason. Who asked you?'

Rossi's cheery sounding solo and the upbeat feel of the music undermine the attack of the words, but the semi-anthemic nature of the song wins out overall. There is a brief section of relative subtlety (2.39-2.53) before the third verse and chorus refrain; 'There never was a better way than living like the way I've done, oh, and living is the game 'til the very last time has come'.

In the coda, the subtle bars appear again (3.44) and the actual ending is the only disappointment. It is weak, informal, and the song would have been much better served by a strong three quaver punch (matching the rhythm and aggressive tone of the title), and a dead stop. Instead, we get three 9th chords that rise chromatically, a clichéd drum fill, and a half-hearted, power chord push.

'Your Smiling Face' (Bown/Parfitt) Duration: 4.22 Chord Count: 5

'Your Smiling Face' is a typical Parfitt rock stomper, medium of pace and unrelenting of rhythm. Lyrically it's your typical 'man begging woman for forgiveness having been caught cheating' blues. We only get to hear the man's perspective, the lady's response is not revealed.

The song is the first step down in the quality level. There's a melodic introduction with plenty of piano against the pretty guitar arpeggios, but once the rhythm section kicks in, that's pretty much it. At over four minutes, the track becomes tedious. A brisker tempo, some greater textural variation, or the loss of a chorus would have made it less mundane.

Rossi has a Chuck Berry-esque solo, and the opening prettiness reappears briefly at 2.46 before the jagged opening riff again punctures the relative calm. There's some backing singing on the chorus refrain, 'I know we made mistakes, had some minor breaks, but the song remains the same, and I need to see your smiling face again'. Rossi reprises his Berry tribute as the song plods off into the fade. 'Your Smiling Face' is to *Whatever You Want* what 'Nightride' was to *On The Level*; adequate but outclassed by the majority of the rest of the album.

'Living On An Island' (Parfitt/Young) Duration: 4.49 Chord Count: 14

The band's first ballad single since moving to Vertigo is a deceptively complex composition. The relaxed strumming of the beautifully recorded acoustic guitar, and Bown's soft keyboard tones, suit the supposedly holiday feel of its words perfectly. But 'Living On An Island' has a darker undertone, and references loneliness and drug abuse in apparently idyllic surroundings. Parfitt's words are semi-autobiographical as he had lived temporarily in the Channel Islands.

Lancaster's bass joins in for the second verse, with the telling lyrics, 'Living on an island, working on another line, waiting for my friend to come and we'll get high' which are again decorated with excellent vocal harmonies. The bridge section, 'Passing time away in blue skies, thinking of the smile in her eyes, easy, it's easy' is equally melodic, and the music then modulates from A to B major where it stays for the rest of the song. The third verse is harmonised and then quietens, pausing at the end of the line 'Waiting for my friend to come and we'll get...*high*' at 2.16.

This, in effect, signifies the beginning of the play-out section, where the instruments and voices combine in a lengthy and impressive coda. Bown's synthesizer melody is memorable as the texture increases and, by the time the song starts to disappear, we are in the middle of an effective instrumental, driven by an understated rhythm section.

'Living On An Island' is a satisfying surprise, and the decision to release it as the second single was a sound one. The song highlights the tuneful, non-rocking side of Quo in a way that the dismal ballads on *Rocking...* and ... *Heat...* utterly failed to achieve.

'Come Rock With Me' (Rossi/Frost) Duration: 3.17 Chord Count: 6

'Come Rock With Me' and 'Rockin' On' are really two sides of the same musical coin, and recall both the joined compositions of 'Is It Really Me' and 'Gotta Go Home', and the mid-section of 'Forty Five Hundred Times', where the straight-eight rhythm moved into a shuffle variant with impressive results.

Neither 'Come Rock With Me' nor 'Rockin' On' has a guitar solo section, relying instead on chord progressions as instrumental interludes. Both tracks are in the same key (B major), and each relies on the hypnotic effect of a great groove played with *élan*. The lyrical theme for both songs is the passing of time, and the fact that, despite the odds, the band are still working and successful.

'Come Rock With Me' is the straight heads-down rocker with Rossi singing against a relentlessly heavy groove. Harmony vocals add shine to the chorus, with the guitars playing off each other to glorious effect. The instrumental has a weighty bass and drum rhythm, with Rossi and Parfitt synchronising together perfectly. It's brief, powerful, and effective, and the song effortlessly segues into…

'Rockin' On' (Rossi/Frost) Duration: 3.22 Chord Count: 6

…a great Quo shuffle, with a fabulously melodic guitar fill as a recurring motif. In the introduction, there is an excellent but far too short, syncopated section followed by a rapid ascending triplet run which is, sadly, not used again. 'Rockin' On' is the band back, thankfully, close to their best. Bown's organ is heard clearly in the background, supporting rather than smothering, and the whole song has a raucous, celebratory sound. Unison backing vocals strengthen the chorus and, again, a guitar chord sequence serves as an instrumental break in the vocals. Towards the end of the track, Lancaster plays an effective descending chromatic run following Coghlan's pick up fill (3.00) into a return of the groove and a quick fade.

'Runaway' (Rossi/Frost) Duration: 4.36 Chord Count: 5

Another brisk rocker, 'Runaway', has similarities to 'Shady Lady' but goes on for about a minute longer than it needs to. It's on the commercial side of melodic, in a major key, and drives along effectively, but it's less involving than the other songs on the album and finds itself sitting alongside 'Your Smiling Face' as another Lower Division number.

The closing instrumental play-out has an irritating fairground style keyboard melody rising to the surface, and there's another short descending bass run as the song fades away. 'Runaway' is the most overtly pop-rock song on the album and would serve as a virtual template for the post 'Frantic Four' version of Quo releases. Here it smells like filler.

'High Flyer' (Lancaster/Young) Duration: 3.51 Chord Count: 4

A rare collaboration between bassist and soon-to-be-departed lyricist results in another commercial song with added clout. There's another regretful lyric about the life of a rock and roller, including 'Here we go another twenty-four hours, every one of them away from you', and 'And in the night when you see the sun, I'm just a face in a crowd of people who want to tell me I'm the only one'.

'High Flyer' is a medium tempo major key groover with Lancaster taking the vocals. There are plenty of strong melodies built into this road-friendly anthem, and backing vocals and keyboards all contribute to a sonic wall of sound. Overall, however, 'High Flyer' is again merely adequate. The bridge (2.14- 2.33) is the most compelling part, and Rossi follows it with a brief solo as the song moves into its final chorus and the eventual fade.

'Breaking Away' (Parfitt) Duration: 6.39 Chord Count: 5

The Parfitt Rock Machine churns out another excellent album closer, this one, whilst also joining two songs together, cements the fact that the band had still 'got it'.

Opening with punchy power chords and some neat guitar interplay, a wonderfully funky riff appears, and we are in 'That's A Fact' territory again, with Bown's keyboard adding some nice chordal touches. It's another 'life on the road' lyric, with an interesting chord sequence underneath the chorus words, 'But I'm changing my tune now, and I'm breaking away'. At 1.55, there's a return to the opening interplay before a determined, rocking groove appears, bass and drums pound in, and the second song just explodes with Parfitt's vocals at 2.44. It's the clever use of tension building and controlled dynamics which makes the actual release so effective.

It's a magnificent transition between the two different song styles and powers along superbly. The lyrically depressing theme is restated with the telling lines, 'Looking a good deal better than we'll ever feel again', and 'Old men in boys' clothes, has gone beyond a joke, skin me another, and pass along the whiskey and the coke'. This is Quo returning to the high energy onslaught of 'Mystery Song', and it's a *very* welcome noise. There's no guitar solo and, all too quickly, the introduction is reprised at 3.52, and then we're off back to Funk Land for the final verse and chorus.

But that isn't the end of the track. At 5.08, there's another change of gear as a smooth instrumental shuffle appears, and Bob Young's superb evocative harmonica intertwines with Rossi's bluesy fills. There are some tasteful keyboards in the background amongst the rising guitars as this fantastic track goes into a slow, atmospheric fade.

'Breaking Away' is an excellent round-off track to an album which, at the time, felt like a life raft to the drowning fan. The song combines creativity, power, and melody into a mini suite of music that shows diversity, control, and genuine rock might in one superb package.

Non-Album Tracks

The 2005 reissue of *Whatever You Want* included a demo version of 'Shady Lady', and the single version of 'Living On An Island', which is approximately a minute shorter than the album track.

'Hard Ride' (Lancaster/Green) Duration: 3.33 Chord Count: 6

This was the B-side to 'Whatever You Want', and it's another fast-paced, major key-centric, commercially aware, little rocker. The repeating guitar phrase is lifted straight from 'Doctor Robert' from *Revolver* by The Beatles, and 'Hard Ride' is all fairly standard, mundane stuff until the instrumental at 2.07. This moves into half tempo and features more excellent harmonica playing from Bob Young. The song then speeds back to repeated choruses, a brief reprise of the introduction, and a fade. Underwhelming.

'Bad Company' (Lancaster) Duration: 4.27 Chord Count: 10

'Bad Company' is an excellent, medium speed groover that cleverly juxtaposes its numerous chord changes over a continuous pedal bass note. Far superior to both 'Your Smiling Face' and 'Runaway', it is another major key song with plenty of melodic highlights both in the vocal lines and the instrumental sections. There's controlled aggression behind the strong melody and steady rhythm over which Rossi's vocals soar, backed by impressive backing vocals. If this was a song Phonogram rejected from the album, they were well off the mark. Lancaster latterly commented in a telephone conversation transcribed in the sleeve notes of the four-disc *Rockers Rollin* compilation album (2002);

> I wrote that for the *Whatever You Want* album, but it was rejected for another track. The song featured an eighteen string guitar belonging to Pip Williams, who I think played it on the track. It's a great track and could still be used today.

Well said. A heavily phased guitar underpins the track mixed in with some acoustic guitar, sustaining keyboards and a deep central groove. 'Bad Company' is lyrically dark; 'You're the witch in the wild, and you're driving me out of my mind, you're the devil inside, I'd rather go blind', and 'I've seen the snake that turned away and lives beneath the moon, and you, you call the tune, you're bad company'. The track successfully mixes a strong commercial melody with an excellent groove and power to produce a song, which deserved far greater exposure than being latterly tacked on as a bonus track 26 years later. But not all bonus tracks are gems...

'Another Game In Town' (Rossi/Frost) Duration: 2.19 Chord Count: 6

Although presented in a rough sounding demo form, this is another up-tempo, upbeat rock-meets-country song with harmonised vocals and a catchy guitar introduction. It's like listening to The Everly Brothers on steroids. Or possibly The Wombles on speed.

'Another Game In Town' is credited to Rossi and Frost, but it sounds more like Young's lyrical contribution with the twisting wordplay in the bridge section (1.12-1.29); 'Two timer, three timer, insider, outside, why do you do it all? Fast runner, slow runner, home runner, lone runner, don't look back it might disturb you, don't let a thing disturb you'. The song really is nothing special and is another strong hint for the sort of flabby, weak and uninspired material the 'reformed' Quo would push on an apparently uncritical public for decades to come.

'Rearrange' (Rossi/Frost) Duration: 3.03 Chord Count: 9
Another demo, another country heavy song decorated with acoustic guitar, laid back bass, and plenty of commercially pop catchiness, which does the band no favours. Vocal harmonies and pleasant melodies abound, but it's still three minutes of your listening life wasted.

Just Supposin…

Personnel:

Francis Rossi

Richard Parfitt

Alan Lancaster

John Coghlan

Guest musicians:

Andy Bown: keyboards and backing vocals

Bob Young: harmonica

Bernie Frost: backing vocals.

Produced by Status Quo and John Eden

Recorded at Windmill Lane Studios, Dublin

Released on 25 October 1980

Highest chart position: 4

Weeks on chart: 18

Before *Just Supposin*… appeared, Vertigo released the superbly titled *'Twelve Gold Bars'* on 22 March 1980, a compilation of the band's single chart successes for the label, consisting of:

'Rocking All Over The World'

'Down Down'

'Caroline'

'Paper Plane'

'Break The Rules'

'Again And Again'

'Mystery Song'

'Roll Over Lay Down'

'Rain'

'Wild Side Of Life'

'Whatever You Want'

'Living On An Island'

The album rose to number three in the UK charts, where it stayed for 48 weeks, a longer run than any other Quo album. The only anomaly was the inclusion of the studio version of 'Roll Over Lay Down' (from *Hello!* which was never released as a single,) instead of the hit live EP recording. The album's success proved to be a double-edged sword, as rumours began to circulate that the band were about to split up. *Twelve Gold Bars* was interpreted as being an end of career retrospective. This was not the case, but there was continuing friction with each member having their own ideas of the direction Quo's music should take. This, together with the degree of substance abuse, was having a distinct effect on the quality of the song writing. There's a fine line between creativity and replication, and *Just Supposin*… had little of the former and too much of the latter.

Work began in February 1980. This time Quo decided to return to self-producing, although the services of John Eden were retained. The sessions were so productive that the band ended up with enough material for either a double vinyl release or, the preferred option, the issue of another new album only five months later. *Just Supposin…* was, however, Bob Young's swansong as he had decided to leave. Looking back on this period in his autobiography Rossi said:

> The painful part was that just as *Whatever You Want* went rocketing up the charts towards the end of 1979, the band was nose-diving in the opposite direction. Jean (Rossi's wife) had already left me, Rick was ill, Alan was in Australia, and John was pretty sick of all of us by that point, by all accounts. Then, early in 1980, with our touring commitments on hold, while Rick got better, Bob announced he was leaving. He'd had enough of the behind the scenes ructions. If I'm being honest, my attitude at the time was very much of the 'good riddance to bad rubbish' variety. I believed he had betrayed me by slagging me off behind my back. Bob believed the same about me. We had both been played for fools.

The album cover is unusual. Against a beautiful ocean backdrop, a guided missile has been launched from, presumably, a submarine and is on a diagonal trajectory upwards whilst a swimmer is passing it going in the opposite direction. The good news was that, despite the oceanic backdrop, there was no sign of any penguin abuse here. On the rear of the single sleeve design is a circle with four individual shots of Lancaster, Parfitt, Rossi, and Coghlan in full flight, sweaty live mode, over the same tranquil ocean painting from the front cover. Strangely, Andy Bown still only warrants a guest credit, and no photograph, despite having been an integral member of the band for several years and co-writer of several significant songs.

Just Supposin… continues the now-familiar trend of strong commercial undertones to various rock hued numbers. Whilst the sound is full and lively with the guitars well to the fore, the quality of the song writing is now in near-terminal decline. There are two good rockers, and some borderline acceptable pop-rocky commercial tracks. On the minus side, two songs are nowhere near good enough, and the inclusion of a mawkish, insipid ballad as a closer just causes the mood to drop even further.

Whatever You Want had got far more about going for it in nearly all departments than this decidedly disappointing follow up. Yes, *Just Supposin…* has a brighter, more engaging production tone than its mid-rangy predecessor, but, as always, it's the songs that matter the most. Whilst the decision to self produce, with John Eden's additional contribution, was a good one, the majority of the material here is either sub-standard or, more damningly, predictable and formulaic. The fact that I only ever want to listen to 'Over The Edge' and 'The Wild Ones' (with an occasional detour into 'What You're

Proposing', because it's just *so* damned catchy), as opposed to nearly all of *Whatever You What* speaks volumes. The few good tracks are *really* good, but there are just nowhere near enough of them, and the propensity for writing unchallenging boppy little pop-rock numbers seems to have taken precedence.

'What You're Proposing' (Rossi/Frost) Duration: 4.15 Chord Count: 6

'What You're Proposing', the first single from the album, was released on 11 October 1980 and reached number two during its eleven-week run. This was the band's best chart showing since 'Down Down', only being denied the top spot by Barbara Streisand's own heavy rock classic 'A Woman In Love'.

References to 'runny nosing' in the nonsensical word play emphasise Rossi's addiction to cocaine at this time. Parfitt and Lancaster were also users, whilst Coghlan, the outsider, preferred alcohol, specifically beer. At the time, Rossi doubted whether he was even capable of writing songs unless under the influence of the drug, hence the line 'I'll get it right if I'm composing, but then I might be runny nosing'.

Critics were delighted to discover that, apart from the fifteen-second instrumental section (which featured some pleasingly harmonised guitars *a la* Thin Lizzy), the rest of the song revolved around the use of just two chords. The rhythm is relentless, the vocal melodies are memorably melodic, and the play-out guitar carries on the catchiness. 'What You're Proposing' had chart success written through it like seaside rock, but it's a long way down from the integrity and commitment of 'Paper Plane', 'Caroline', 'Down Down', or 'Rain'.

'Run To Mummy' (Rossi/Bown) Duration: 3.10 Chord Count: 8

Continuing the recent theme of having an upbeat major-key second track, 'Run To Mummy' is another driving pop-rocker with a strong commercial feel amongst all the powerful playing. Lancaster and Bown's contributions are both busy and well mixed around Rossi's double-tracked vocals. Lyrically the song deals with the hypocrisy that can be found in some relationships. Musically it's just another below average, post *Rocking...*, Quo song. There is neither space nor time for a guitar solo, and the track soon goes into a fade.

'Don't Drive My Car' (Bown/Parfitt) Duration: 4.36 Chord Count: 7

'Don't Drive My Car' was the second single from the album, released as a double A-side with 'Lies', on 6 December 1980. It was, however, this track which took hold in the record buying public's consciousness as the single got as far as number 10 during an eleven-week run.

There is the unwelcome return to the overcrowded production values of ... *Heat...* in this saggy, funk-meets-rock, inspiration-lite dirge. There are some cheap-sounding keyboards, an over-reliance on reverb, and lyrically it's either tongue-in-cheek rubbish or foot-in-mouth clumsiness. This is Parfitt in 'Alpha

Male Mode', and his rough-toned vocal style is more suited to the outright rockers rather than this dross. The repeated 'oh, oh, oh, oh' refrain quickly becomes an irritation, and the track outstays its very limited welcome by well over a minute.

An instrumental section features some swirling synths underneath a rising chord progression, then Rossi lets loose with an uninspiring solo before Parfitt's barky vocal style returns. The play out has a heavily processed guitar solo over what sounds like some flacid synth drum sounds. It's all very busy, and was no doubt considered a good idea at the time, but a better title would be 'Don't Play This Song'.

'Lies' (Rossi/Frost) Duration: 4.01 Chord Count: 4

And now it's time for some countrified pub-rock. Why? Don't know.

'Lies' is an unexceptional chugger, replete with double-tracked Rossi vocals, some irritating high pitched backing vocals, another major key, and another medium tempo. Both the verse and the chorus melodies are yet again commercial and catchy, and Bown's organ fills out the backing instrumentation, but there's nothing remotely special going on here. The absence of a guitar solo means the ears soon get bored with a song that does nothing with dynamics, or changes in texture, as it rolls on, and on, and on, into a welcome fade.

'Over The Edge' (Lancaster/Lamb) Duration: 4.30 Chord Count: 6

Ladies and gentlemen, will you please welcome…a Proper. Rock. Song!

'Over The Edge' is magnificent and blows the rest of *Just Supposin*… clean out of the water. It's heavy, unrelenting, and supremely powerful. Lancaster's singing is fine and gruff, the chorus is uplifting and anthemic, and the band sound, for the first time on this record, on fire. Borrowing the idea of a repeated bass pedal groove with rising chords from 'Oh What A Night', *everything* is right about this song, and even the heroic sounding *keyboard* solo (2.29-2.43) sounds great. Yes, you did read that last sentence correctly.

Lancaster's co-composer for this epic rocker was Keith Lamb, lead singer of Australian band Hush. This, their sole contribution, is far more welcome than yet another Rossi/Frost bouncily cheery pop-rock composition. How can this one song sound *so* good and the rest of the album be so lame by comparison? It's the first and only really good track on the album.

'Over The Edge' would justifiably become a fixture in the live set-list and can be heard on 1984's *'Live At The NEC'*, where it's taken at a slightly faster tempo but still remains monumentally heavy, determined, and aggressive. It's been said that the song was a personal favourite of HRH Prince Charles despite the fact he believed it to be called 'Over The Hedge', an understandable error what with him not being a 'Sarf London Boy'. The studio version's fade is replaced with a sudden vicious bar of drum triplets to come to a sudden stop. An instant classic and, sadly, a song that stands out as being the last great number the band would produce between this album and their disintegration four years in the future.

'The Wild Ones' (Lancaster) Duration: 4.01 Chord Count: 7

A major key Celtic-style low string riff sets this 'Son Of 'Over The Edge'' track going over another shuffling bass pedal note groove with the chords shifting position above it. Bown's Hammond organ adds an early 1970s rock sound to the verse, whilst the chorus has a greater melodic and commercial feel to it. Lancaster's role as the only member of the band seemingly determined to write some true rockers remains undiminished. However, there are too many keyboards in the song's mix, Rossi's main vocal line is yet again double-tracked, and there is no guitar solo or instrumental interlude to break things up. Nevertheless, 'The Wild Ones' remains one of only three good tracks in this collection.

At 1.56, the song enters a new section which could have become a separate track in its own right; 'I remember the summertime and the riding out into the breeze, and I remember the apple wine, filling my head with dreams if only I could walk away'. But the easy riders (drug dealers) are 'coming, but now there's somebody gone, I'm sitting here all alone, looking away, looking away'. This is another example of up-beat music having much darker lyrical concerns. The key has modulated from E to A major and takes the form of a traditional twelve-bar before a series of gear crunching key changes brings the introduction back at 2.50. The play-out features some highly recognisable Rossi string bends as the song fades away into the distance.

'Name Of The Game' (Bown/Lancaster/Rossi) Duration: 4.34 Chord Count: 7

This is the only composition by Bown, Lancaster, and Rossi, and what a hotchpotch it is. 'Name Of The Game' is notable for all the wrong reasons with too much involved instrumentation, an absence of real energy or commitment, and an unspectacular lyrical and musical performance. Somehow it manages to get on the nerves almost as soon as it starts.

The introduction is the best part of the song; chiming chords are punctuated by short rhythmic stabs, but it quickly lapses into a chugging rhythm that never seems to either settle or, paradoxically, get going. 'Name Of The Game' is an ear-itating track; there are the, by now, compulsory harmonised verse vocals, an annoying refrain, and Bown's organ requires some serious subduing. There is also a lyrical nod to 'I Shot The Sheriff' by Bob Marley. Why?

At 2.02, a short and yet still uninspiring solo drifts on by in a new key which quickly modulates back to the introduction and the third verse and chorus. Then there's a long and tiresome fade, with the irksome 'I didn't do it, I did not do it' refrain being endlessly repeated, as Bown's keyboards stretch the listener's patience close to breaking point.

'Coming And Going' (Parfitt/Young) Duration: 6.31 Chord Count: 8

The longest song on the album by a country mile, 'Coming And Going' is also the last time Bob Young's emotive harmonica playing would feature on a Quo album. Whilst having an insistent rocking rhythm redolent of the band's longer early 1970s 'jam' songs, this track has too much reverb applied, especially to the vocals, and just goes on. *For. Far. Too. Long.* There's not enough material here to work effectively for six and a half minutes, and the absence of any changes to the instrumentation, dynamics, or tempo eventually puts the mind on pause, waiting for something better to come along. It doesn't, but you never know your luck...

There's a catchy little guitar riff over this bass-heavy mix, and Parfitt's vocal melody in the parallel major key of C major is effective. The chorus has a melodic appeal to it, but that's all this song's got. And stretching it out beyond what could be a reasonably satisfying, but probably space-filling three minutes is really doing the listener's ears a severe disservice. Ultimately 'Coming And Going' is relentless, noisy, and boring.

At the four-minute mark, the song passes its 'pay-attention-to' point of no return. Failing to take the hint, the track then drones on, and I mean *really* drones on, for a further two minutes without invention, creativity, or inspiration. Eventually, it fades away, and by this point, I had just stopped caring, and was grateful for the eventual silence. It was to be a short-lived peace...

'Rock N Roll' (Rossi/Frost) Duration: 5.25 Chord Count: 8

Rossi's confessional lightweight ballad may have been an attempt to ape Parfitt's far superior 'Living On An Island'. 'Rock N Roll', grammatical errors notwithstanding, is an awful, awful song.

Acoustic guitars, a keyboard set to 'extra cheese', hugely annoying backing vocals, and a lugubrious tempo all contribute to a banal listening experience. 'Rock N Roll' has no redeeming features whatsoever, not a single one. It should be seen as a warning from the future, transported back in time by concerned long-term fans, from when the Rossi and Parfitt Group band would produce *and sell* crud like this on a regular basis. I would rather stick rusty pins in my eyes than have to listen to this dreadful dirge again.

There is a guitar solo from 4.36, which leads to the very welcome fade, but this is only a good thing because it means the dreadful, indulgent lyrics are over, the soppy arrangements are finally in the background, and it can't be too long before this aural abomination is over.

'Rock N Roll' was released as a single on 20 November 1981, *after* the release of the band's next album *Never Too Late* (and the first single from it, 'Somethin' Bout You Baby I Like') and somehow managed to limp up to number eight in the charts. Sickly sweet, self-indulgent, and packed full of coma-inducing dullness, the song proved just how poor Quo would become when they attempted to swim in the mainstream and appeal to the masses.

Non-Album Track
'AB Blues (Instrumental)' (Bown/Rossi/Parfitt/Lancaster/Coghlan)
Duration: 4.25 Chord Count: 3

This was the B-side to 'What You're Proposing' and is only the second instrumental the band had released.

A three-chord bluesy jam that surely didn't take five people to write, 'AB Blues (Instrumental)' starts mid-phrase and is medium of tempo throughout. It meanders along easily enough, nothing much happens, and you begin to wonder what the point of it is. The lead lines are shared between Parfitt and Rossi, and from 3.50 they harmonise in the style of The Allman Brothers to the fade. It's something to listen to whilst the first coat of magnolia dries, I suppose.

Never Too Late

Personnel:
Francis Rossi
Richard Parfitt
Alan Lancaster
John Coghlan
Guest musicians:
Andy Bown: keyboards and backing vocals
Bernie Frost: backing vocals.
Produced by Status Quo and John Eden.
Recorded at Windmill Lane Studios, Dublin
Released on 28 March 1981
Highest chart position: 2
Weeks on chart: 13

The 'leftovers' album, or if you prefer, an overspill collection from the prolific (in quantity, if not quality) *Supposin...* sessions is, on balance, better than its predecessor. All the songs were recorded in Dublin at the same time as the *Supposin...* tracks, and this 'twin' album was released just five months later.

The linking of *Supposin...* and *Never Too Late* is not just down to the close proximity of their launches. The new album's cover artwork, credited to Chris Moore, continued the missile theme. Here we have a view of the Earth from space and a disembodied hand holding a missile (not the same one as on the *Supposin...* sleeve), possibly preventing its return to the planet. The familiar band logo is in a small font in the top right corner and the album title looks like it's been tagged on as an afterthought in the bottom left.

On the rear of the single sleeve, the four members are seen as ghostly beings floating amongst the stars, smiling Rock Gods, if you will. This image was strictly for the camera; seemingly no one was enjoying being in Status Quo anymore. Again, Andy Bown gets a guest musician credit, but not a picture, despite being a co-writer of three of the ten tracks. Coghlan, Rossi, Parfitt and Lancaster are all listed by name but not instrument.

Never Too Late was really the beginning of the end for the line-up. Coghlan would leave during the sessions for the next album. Bob Young, an intrinsic part of both the band's management and song-writing teams for the past decade, had gone. And the inclusion of two cover versions didn't project the image of a band at the peak of their creative powers.

Sound-wise, *Never Too Late* is less involving and harder work to listen to than *Supposin...*; it is mushy, mid-rangy, and less compelling. The vocals and lead guitar are, generally, not as far forward in the mix as they should be, and the songs almost exclusively feature the double-tracked Rossi vocals, so the variety that a Parfitt or Lancaster-fronted number would bring is missing. There are a couple of interesting production tricks pulled on what was the second side of the album, and, fortunately, no one felt the need to contribute a syrupy ballad.

This led to a meatier and more satisfying effort. However, a really good slower song would have improved the structure of the album's sequencing. As it is, *Never Too Late* is all a bit relentless and wearing on the ears. There's not enough light and shade, and the songs and the sound tend to merge into one another.

Of course, by now, there was the underlying commerciality to most of the tracks, and this was now seemingly accepted by fans as the default setting for the band. Overall the actual songs here are superior to those on *Supposin...* with plenty of drive, some clever invention, and lots of energy. There isn't a stand-out number to match 'Over The Edge', but, equally, there's less dross, and a more even consistency of melodic rockers. And there's the rub for both albums. Neither could be described as essential Quo, but equally, they are nowhere near as forgettable, disposable, and disappointing as this line-up's final two releases. Both *Just Supposin'* and *Never Too Late* operate at a cruising altitude. It's all downhill from here.

'Never Too Late' (Rossi/Frost) Duration: 4.00 Chord Count: 6

This melodic chugger regrettably sets the template for much of what will follow for the next 41 minutes. Some dramatic, rapid-fire, staccato chords open proceedings, but then we're quickly into a comfortable medium tempo, major key number. Rossi's vocals lament the state of the world but hold out hope for the future. There's a brief instrumental interlude into the third verse, which is, unimaginatively, a retread of the opening lyrics, and the main guitar solo (1.06-1.20) leads into the bridge section; 'Now this old sea dog's gonna get away across the water...'.

There's a repeat of the introduction where the lead vocals are joined by high pitched and close-miked backing singers, which quickly become intrusive. A repeat of the bridge doesn't manage to jettison the backing vocals overboard, which leads into the play out of this unremarkable track. There's very little by way of dynamic or textural alterations, and, whilst all the requisite Quo trademarks are present, the band sound tired. The opening track of an album shouldn't sound like filler, but this one manages it effortlessly as it slowly fades away.

'Something 'Bout You Baby I Like' (Supa) Duration: 2.51 Chord Count: 5

It was the country music interpretation of Richard Supa's song by Glen Campbell and Rita Coolidge which prompted Rossi to want to cover the track and give it the 'Quo Treatment'. The end result certainly sounds like a Quo song *of this period*. Prior to *Rocking...* this poppy bopper wouldn't have got a look in, but standards have slipped, and obvious commercialism has crept in, to the extent that this barely adequate track was given second billing. 'Something 'Bout You Baby I Like', backed with 'Enough Is Enough', was the first single to be issued from the album and rose to number nine in the charts on an eleven-week run.

It's a typical Quo interpretation. Rossi sings the opening couplet, Parfitt takes the next two lines, and the pair sings in unison for the refrain. For the second verse, there's some choral style 'ooh' backing vocals, and then we're into a full-bodied instrumental with the lead guitar too far back in mix. A third verse and refrain then moves into the coda section with repeated 'Yeah, yeah, there's something 'bout you baby I like's, finally fading away. But there's very little distinction between the instruments, and there's no dynamic alteration, so the ears soon get bored even though the toes tap to the insidious rhythm. It's a very busy sound, and when it's finished, it's a relief.

'Take Me Away' (Bown/Parfitt) Duration: 4.48 Chord Count: 9

This is more like it. Opening with some guitar interplay not far removed from 'Hold You Back', 'Take Me Away' is a thunderous shuffle with some committed playing and a tightly rocking groove throughout. It's proud, noisy, and means business. The lyrics again reference the burnout the band was approaching: 'A mental disaster, a physical wreck, get me away from here. The glamorous lifestyle sure is a pain in the neck, so get me away from here'.

On the debit side, Rossi's vocals seem to have been recorded from inside a deep well, and, again, there's no dynamic light and shade in the song. However, the positives are weightier; the chorus is anthemic and the guitar solo (1.47-2.26) over a relentless C minor rhythm brings to mind the long instrumental section of 'Umleitung'. Here Rossi plays with real feel and attack as if he's just remembered that Quo are at their best when they are genuinely rocking, as opposed to throwing out lightweight boogie patiently assembled for mass audience consumption. The introduction is reprised before the third verse and chorus and a play-out solo (3.24 to the end) where Rossi once again delivers the goods.

'Falling In Falling Out' (Bown/Parfitt/Young) Duration: 4.15 Chord Count: 8

And as if one really good rocker is enough, the band now put their pop trousers back on again for this (here come those words again…) up-tempo, catchy, major key stomper. 'Falling In Falling Out' is not without invention; Lancaster's bass cleverly uses octave notes under the verse, and the pre-chorus ('Standing in line again, wasting my time, I know I'd feel fine again, with you on the line…') has a half-tempo reggae feel to it. It's an effective change enabling the next section to have a greater effect on the listener.

The chorus is both ridiculous and ridiculously catchy. As seems to be the *modus operandi* for this album, Rossi's vocals are yet again double-tracked, and the key modulates briefly to D major for his solo (2.47- 3.06). There is a shift through the musical gears to land back into the original key of A major for the play out, which is the repeated chorus, with Bown's quaver violin sound stabs dominating the fade.

'Carol' (Berry) Duration: 3.35 Chord Count: 10

The last time the band covered a Chuck Berry song was, of course, 'Bye Bye Johnny', and here they serve up another thunderous three and a half minutes, this time of one of his less familiar tunes. The original, dating from 1958, sounds very quaint in comparison to Quo's version. This is an out-and-out twelve-bar rocker that is powerful, loud, and is not collecting any prisoners en route. The band's capacity for rejuvenating the usual formula is on display here. Unlike Berry's composition, Quo's 'Carol' modulates from B major to D major for the instrumental section, and changes again to C major for the remainder of the song. It blasts along, however, without 'Johnny's effective dynamic variation for its duration.

'Long Ago' (Rossi/Frost) Duration: 3.48 Chord Count: 6

What starts out as a sort of cross between a slowed down 'What You're Proposing' and a more interesting rewrite of 'Never Too Late' again shows some minor levels of creativity.

Beginning with country-esque guitar bends, the song soon moves into a straight four-to-the-floor mid-tempo stomper. We have the seemingly inevitable Rossi vocals and, at the pre-chorus 'You'd better hold on a minute, wait for a minute, don't leave me on my knees', the song slides into 3/4 time for four bars, before lapsing back into 4/4 for the second verse. When the chorus arrives, the music subtly moves into an effective shuffle rhythm before falling back into a straight crotchet beat for the next verse and shuffling chorus. There is no space or time for a solo; the play-out consists of repeated lines from the first verse, interspersed with 'la la la' backing vocals which are too high up in the mix as the song fades away.

'Mountain Lady' (Lancaster) Duration: 5.05 Chord Count: 9

'Mountain Lady' motors along with a sense of joyous abandon and is one of Lancaster's typically melodic, road-friendly songs. Again the track is set in a major key, with prominent keyboards, Rossi vocals, and catchy melodies throughout. There's an interesting syncopation and submerged keyboard arpeggios underlying the 'I'm taking a walk in your heart' section (1.03-1.16), and the instrumental (2.22-2.48) is strong and tuneful. The bridge, 'There's never been a better reason at any time before,' has strong pop undertones in both the chord progression and the vocal harmonies.

The introduction returns with a repeat of the syncopated section before another run through the instrumental with Bown making his presence heard. Bizarrely the track neither fades nor comes to a live ending; halfway through the repeated chord instrumental, the song is abruptly cut off, crashing us straight into…

'Don't Stop Me Now' (Bown/Lancaster) Duration: 3.40 Chord Count: 6

Another fast, urgent-sounding track, 'Don't Stop Me Now' is a stormer that features the suspended fourth/major third harmonic movement to the same great effect as the instrumental sections of 'Mountain Lady', the refrain of 'Whatever You Want', and, of course, the famous guitar melody of 'Caroline'.

The song grooves away relentlessly with more harmonised vocals which have too much reverb applied to them, and sound too far back in the mix as a consequence. The music changes key from D to F major for its keyboard-heavy instrumental section before a return to the relentless and hypnotic central riff. This track is like a hyperactive steamroller, it just keeps going, but, again, the lack of changes in instrumentation, arrangement, or dynamics fail to make it anything other than a great foot-tapping mood lifter. The song is well titled but, aside from the obvious energy and seemingly endless central riff, there isn't much else to mark it out as distinctive.

'Enough Is Enough' (Rossi/Frost/ Parfitt) Duration: 2.53 Chord Count: 5

Another jaunty, up-tempo, foot-tapper with Rossi taking centre vocal stage *yet again*, 'Enough Is Enough', bizarrely, comes across as an old-fashioned London pub 'knees up' on performance-enhancing drugs. I don't want to type the words 'Chas' and 'Dave' here, but it looks like I'm going to have to, as it's not too much of a reach to imagine this being covered by the 'rockney' duo who were enjoying a brief period of pop-chart fame around this time.

This is another major-key commercially melodic little rocker, with a further weird twist at 1.45 when we get a fairground sounding keyboard solo. I say 'solo'; it's just the same nine note phrase played eight times. Presciently the song fades on repeats of the refrain. 'Enough is enough, I can't stand no more, enough is enough, I can't anymore'. In the fade, the tempo increases dramatically as if the song itself wants to get out of the studio. I know how it feels.

'Riverside' (Rossi/Frost) Duration: 5.10 Chord Count: 6

A number packed with plenty of production trickery, 'Riverside' is the same song done in two different ways blended together into one track. It fades in on the 'Riverside' refrain in the key of F major with a medium shuffle setting, which is shoved to one side by the main version, a straight-ahead rocker in B flat major, 25 seconds in.

The music shifts briefly into C major and then back into B flat major for an instrumental (0.55-1.11), which cleverly throws in a bar of 5/4 time under the drum syncopation in its twelfth and final bar before we're back into the next verses. At 1.35, a bridge section briefly emerges: 'Don't blame me, don't point your finger at me…', which is still heavy and commercial, before the return of the instrumental at 1.56, this time staying in D major. Verse vocals resume in C major, as does the bridge section, and there's a repeat of the first instrumental. At 3.08, the song changes musical gear yet again.

The rest of the number is the slower tempo shuffle rhythm which opened the track. The vocal refrain gradually moves into the background of this sonic mush as Bown's violin keyboards rise to prominence in the long, long fade with synth drums and guitars battling for space in the mix. Solo free and yet, again, seemingly unable to show any musical creativity, the band should have picked one of the versions of the song and stuck with it. They might have come up with something more akin to the mighty 'Breaking Away' from *Whatever You Want*. As it is, the words 'dog's' and 'breakfast' spring to mind, and stay there...

1+9+8+2

Personnel:
Francis Rossi: Guitar, lead and backing vocals
Richard Parfitt: Guitar, lead and backing vocals
Alan Lancaster: Bass guitar, lead and backing vocals
Andy Bown: Keyboards and backing vocals
Pete Kircher: Drums, percussion, and backing vocals
Guest musician:
Bernie Frost: backing vocals
Produced by Status Quo
Engineered by Dave Richards
Recorded at Mountain Studios, Montreux, Switzerland
Released on 24 April 1982
Highest chart position: 1
Weeks on chart: 20

Whilst the music industry was busy celebrating twenty years of Status Quo, the mood within the band was far from positive. By now The Frantic Four were reduced to three following the sudden departure of John Coghlan, which was a massive blow to both band and fans.

During recording sessions for the new album the notoriously moody drummer apparently kicked his kit over, walked out of the studio, and flew home to the Isle of Man. Coghlan had felt excluded from the drug taking triumvirate of Rossi, Parfitt and Lancaster for years. Whatever the specific final straw was, what was more worrying and indicative of the state of the Quo was that nobody tried to stop him, or even persuade him to return. In an interview with *Record Mirror* at the time Rossi's view was:

> It could have been any one of us (to quit). I don't think John was planning to leave the band as such; it isn't something you plan for. But he had been thinking and talking about it for some time.

The guitarist recalled the events in his autobiography:

> I used to joke that the reason John left was because his pet hates were gigging, rehearsing, and recording. Which was not fair. John was a great drummer and long term fans now understandably regard that line-up as the classic one. The truth is the whole shebang was out of control at the time John packed it in. We all threw huge wobblers at different times. But nobody ever came over and put their arm around your shoulder. They just left you to it. I was probably the worst for that. I didn't want to know about anybody else's problems. I had too many of my own. We all did. Something that was borne out by the fact that we all bailed out not long after.

Quoted in the CD inlay booklet accompanying the 2018 CD reissue Coghlan said of the situation;

> I had too much to drink and, allegedly, I was supposed to have kicked the drums over. I was with the band for nearly twenty years, and we never stopped. It's the old story, if we weren't rehearsing, then we were recording, and if we weren't recording, then we were touring. We all know how rock'n'roll works; too much drink, too much of this, too much of that.

Also from the CD booklet is another quotation from another interview the drummer gave;

> ...Things weren't happy for me at home in those days and nobody in the band was too interested in anybody else's problems. If I threw a wobbler about something, or anyone else did, nobody asked why; they just avoided you for a while. It was such a shame, because the original band was shit hot and we allowed it to fall apart.

In the 2016 CD booklet Lancaster described how Coghlan's departure affected the functioning of the band:

> John was a big part of the dynamic. He wasn't a writer, but his drumming was very creative. Once John had gone, each band member was alone, suddenly it was every man for himself whereas previously the four of us had worked together.

Coghlan's replacement was supposed to be a temporary appointment to ensure an album was salvaged from the recording sessions. Rossi suggested Pete Kircher, an experienced session drummer. Kircher's band, Shanghai, had played as support to Quo on the *Blue For You* tour. Upon arrival in Switzerland, Kircher fitted in so well that he was offered the permanent position.

But Quo, without Coghlan's input, was a very different animal, as Lancaster noted in the CD booklet;

> Pete was a great man for the job and a fantastic substitute, but he wasn't John. Pete was subservient, but John came up with his own ideas. It was a big difference. So John was out, and that was the start. It was unthinkable at the time. And it was never the same since. We made bad albums after that.

There was another announcement for the rock press. Andy Bown was *finally* promoted to full band member status after an apprenticeship of a mere five years, hundreds of gigs, and contributing as a writer to eleven songs, including the anthemic hit 'Whatever You Want'. Now that's what I call a probationary period.

114

And it was this revised line-up, The Frantic Three + Two if you like, which gave us this disaster. It's hard to dislike *1+9+8+2,* but it's well worth the effort. Step One: Insert CD into CD player. Step Two: Press play. Step Three: 39 minutes and 20 seconds later, job done.

The album cover is a very formal affair. On a white background, the band's name is in a smart, capitalised blue font with '1+9+8+2' underneath in red. Spoiler alert, twenty is the sum of one, nine, eight and two, the band's anniversary. Two small parallel lines above a black triangle with two white X's indicated the number 20 in Roman numerals. On the rear of the single sleeve cover, there is a band photograph introducing the 'new boys'. Kircher, just in case help was needed, was holding a pair of drumsticks. As if to serve as a warning as to what we about to receive, Rossi was wearing … a brown jumper. This was deeply worrying.

The cover is better than the songs. The band sound like they are pulling or being pulled in too many directions. There are plenty of standard chugging Quo rhythms, but the overall tone is middle-of-the-road pop-rock with few numbers that warrant a second listen. Rossi's vocals feature heavily, newly promoted Bown seems to have been similarly lifted in the mix, not usually to a song's benefit, and there's plenty of high-pitched backing vocals failing to add much shine to these very ordinary offerings. There is also the unwelcome presence of some typical early 1980s production trickery. Years later, Rossi reflected on the album, saying in the CD inlay booklet which accompanied the following album:

> We were trying to change, especially the writing style. There were a lot of changes. We were trying to tidy up the sound, recording techniques were changing and it was a new decade. Looking back, I suppose we were drifting away from the format that we had established.

What *1+9+8+2* lacks is, yet again*, good* songs. It has a few semi-reasonable tracks, but that's all. Three out of eleven isn't a pass rate in anyone's book. The band was by now a shadow of their former mighty selves, and the template for what the post-1985 group would regurgitate for decades to come was almost completely in place. There are the occasional, brief flurries of former glories, but these are, in the main, restricted to the odd good riff here and there. The production lacks power and bite, and some of the tracks are so poor that Quo were in very real danger of turning into pastiches of themselves. Tellingly, the best song of this low rent bunch, 'Dear John', was not composed by the band.

Most surprisingly, *1+9+8+2* was the first Quo album to reach number one in the album chart since *Blue For You,* and would be the last chart-topping album the band would release. It is, at best, an acquired taste. Like brake fluid. Ten years earlier, the band had released *Piledriver*. Just a thought. Unbelievably, worse was yet to come with the band's final fling, as Lancaster observed in the CD reissue sleeve notes:

The image of the band was changing right in front of our eyes and nobody was doing anything about it. Cocaine was endemic and members of the band were no longer getting along, and with me being in Australia, we lost that sense of push and pull. If Francis wanted something then he'd almost certainly get his way because Rick had no one to back him up. For me, the band was already finished before Back To Back ... Status Quo was over and done when John Coghlan left in 1982, only we didn't realise it at the time.

'She Don't Fool Me' (Parfitt/Bown) Duration: 4.34 Chord Count: 10

Some bright major chords with bass counterpoint are played three times and lead into a mid-paced honky-tonk chugger, with Rossi's vocals and Bown's keyboards prominent in the mix. Backing vocals join in for the unexceptional chorus. After a second verse and chorus, the introduction is reprised again with Kircher driving things from the back seat; then we're into the final verse and choruses.

'She Don't Fool Me' is a boppy-poppy rocker that sounds uninspired and formulaic. Because it is. Repeated introductions and some driving bass from Lancaster pick up the 'power-to-(saggy)-weight' ratio very slightly, but as the song goes into a fade, you realise that nothing else of note has happened. It was the second single released from the album and scraped into the Top 40 at number 36.

'Young Pretender' (Rossi/Frost) Duration: 3.32 Chord Count: 8

And it gets no better. 'Young Pretender' has all the same ingredients that made 'She Don't Fool Me' such an attention dodging opener. It's another mid-tempo major key chugger that just drains the listener's will to live as it drones on, and on, and on. Some fashionable-for-the-time keyboards seep through the mix in a desperate attempt to make the song chart-friendly and relevant. Actually, the track is weak and predictable in every department. It's as if Kircher is already turning into a half-man/half drum machine hybrid. Bizarrely 'Young Pretender' sounds like it's a cover version of some dreadful crooner-led ballad from the Sixties set to a shuffle beat. It isn't, but that only means that no one else can be blamed for this aural abomination.

'Get Out And Walk' (Parfitt/Bown) Duration: 3.09 Chord Count: 8

The first song to actually sound like a proper Quo track, starts with a decently aggressively riff over a conventional blues chord sequence which has similarities to 'Oh Baby' from a decade ago. 'Get Out And Walk' soon develops into a reasonable rocker that could have sat comfortably on any of the three Pip Williams era albums. Lancaster throbs away relentlessly at the bottom end, and the chorus, whilst still catchy and commercial, does at least have some balls to it.

All's going well fairly well until we reach the instrumental (1.53-2.06); some sub-Thin Lizzy-esque phased guitars appear as part of a twee little interlude that just doesn't belong here, and the tension and mood are lost. Fortunately, the driving power returns for the introduction, another chorus, and repeated introductions, which are, again, spoilt by keyboard fills. There is a tight ending to the song, but the words 'missed' and 'opportunity' loom large on the horizon.

'Jealousy' (Rossi/Frost) Duration: 2.54 Chord Count: 4

As you were, normal service is now resumed. 'Jealousy' is just as poor as 'Young Pretender', and the two songs are virtually identical in their poppy style, uninspired arrangement, and the growing sense that the band were no longer interested or cared about making good rock music. Medium tempo, major key, massive disappointment. Next.

'I Love Rock And Roll' (Lancaster) Duration: 3.15 Chord Count: 8

If you thought the album had, by now, flat-lined and had nowhere else to fall, think again. Exhibit five in this Museum of Musical Mucus is just dreadful; there really is no other printable word for it. Lancaster is capable of so much better. He may, indeed, 'love rock'n'roll' but this song is to Rock'n'Roll what Boris Johnson is to integrity.

Fans of banal, clichéd lyrics will be delighted by the lack of invention, or indeed *any* spark of creativity here. The chorus is atrocious and sounds like the sort of tiresome rubbish pop-rock lite bands of the mid-Seventies like The Arrows and the Bay City Rollers issued. In the CD inlay booklet, the bassist was later quoted as saying:

> It's one of the worst songs I've written though at the time I thought it was quite clever in a technical sense.

Oh, that's alright then; best put it on the album.

'Resurrection' (Parfitt/Bown) Duration: 3.49 Chord Count: 8

A possibly promising start with slide guitar over a pedal bass shuffle rhythm quickly descends into predictable mediocrity with an alarmingly disposable chorus. The backing vocals alternate between gospel choir style harmonies and the sound of blokes down the pub on the outside of eight pints believing they have discovered the gift of song.

Another medium speed trudge through a creative wasteland, 'Resurrection' opened the second side of the vinyl album. The previously reliable writing of Parfitt and Bown seems caught up in the same delusion as Lancaster; if a song has a shuffle rhythm and references to 'rock and roll', it will be good enough. No. Wrong. Very wrong. This track could have easily sat alongside some of the turgid bilge on …*Heat*… with an equal chance of being just as unmemorable. The only section of partial interest is the instrumental (1.42-2.12), where the second half of the solo is played on slide guitar. Overall, however, this is, yet again, desperately poor.

'Dear John' (Gustafson/Macauley) Duration: 3.12 Chord Count: 6

'Dear John' is a typically robust little groover that encapsulates the rocking commercial face that Quo had wanted their fans to accept since 1977. Rossi's reedy vocals ride above an above-average composition with a compelling chorus and, this time, effective harmony vocals. There are strong elements of country *twang* to the guitar, with a repeated chorus before the final verse, which is a straight repeat of the first and repeated choruses to the fade. 'Dear John' is a solid, second-level Quo track which, when released as a single prior to the album, got to number ten in the charts during its eight-week run. The fact that it is pretty much the best song on the album speaks volumes.

'Doesn't Matter' (Rossi/Frost) Duration: 3.36 Chord Count: 8

'Doesn't Matter' is another lame offering from the Rossi/Frost stable. As it is, it trots along with irrelevant lyrics, backing vocals which make the teeth itch, and an almost complete lack of imagination in its arrangement. The monotony is only broken up with a new section (1.06-1.20, and again at 2.17-2.31) which is slightly heavier. Then there's a swift return to poppy-boppy-blandness, and the song just chugs itself off to its fading end at the nearby glue factory. Close the gate on your way out, would you?

'I Want The World To Know' (Lancaster/Lamb) Duration: 3.23 Chord Count: 15

The only other song on the album to have any sort of rock potential has Lancaster taking over vocal duties with his characteristic rough vocal delivery over a driving rhythm. In a rare instance of putting their best musical eggs in one single basket, 'I Want The World To Know' was the B-side to 'Dear John'.

There's a similarity here to the far superior 'Over The Edge' with the solid pedal bass line. The chorus is half decent and is sung with a degree of authenticity sadly lacking elsewhere. However, the second verse's lyrics have references to 'rocking all over the world' and 'down down', and creativity seems to have packed its bags and gone overseas on a gap year. There's some power behind the chord driven instrumental section before Rossi's solo, which is interrupted by the backing vocals. The overall sound is mushy with too much going on, especially from the keyboards, and much of the song's potential has been produced out of it.

'I Should Have Known' (Rossi/Frost) Duration: 3.30 Chord Count: 8

A rollicking country-style introduction with some surprisingly effective harmonies in the guitar parts and a brisk tempo brings to mind 'Rolling Home' (*Blue For You*). These worthy themes are soon dispensed with, and we're quickly into another country-rock flavoured nonentity. The chorus ups the commercial feel, but not in a good way. Another verse and chorus lead inevitably to a solo, this time mimicking the vocal melody, which turns out to be the beginning of the end for this song as it fades away over a simple repeated guitar motif. By this stage in proceedings, it is not unrealistic to suggest that Quo's contribution to the musical landscape now seems to be the invention of a new sub-genre; 'Lobotomy Rock'. It's like being on the concussion ward at midnight.

'Big Man' (Lancaster/Lamb) Duration: 3.42 Chord Count: 4
Some echoed sound effects approximating a horror film soundtrack lead into a brief funky guitar riff and a leaden, synthesizer-dominated rhythm. The verse drops into half tempo, with Lancaster doing his best to make the infantile, useless words sound sincere and convincing. In the bridge section (1.08, and again at 1.56), his tone and phrasing have a bizarre Roger Waters feel to them, when the Floyd vocalist is set to extra-anguished. The chorus is equally abysmal. For those of us accustomed to Quo albums, even the lesser quality ones, ending with something rousing and powerful, this is a major kick in the teeth, and ears.

The song sounds 'big' in production terms, there's loads going on, plenty of keyboards and electronic percussion sound effects, but none of it ever approaches interesting. If you were asked to name the band playing the track, you wouldn't put Status Quo in the frame. Minimal points, I suppose, for at least trying something different. Nil points, however, for coming up with this. Lancaster at least had the decency to condemn the composition, years after the album's release in the CD inlay booklet:

That was another bloody terrible one. It was supposed to have a completely different groove. We needed a sequencer to make it work, and they still hadn't been invented.

Non-Album Track
'Calling The Shots' (Parfitt/Bown) Duration: 4.56 Chord Count: 12
This song's keyboard-heavy, up-beat introduction sounds like a soundtrack for a middling quality 1980s film, probably starring Rob Lowe. Sung by Bown, it is one of those tracks that the mind purposely forgets while it's hearing it in order to protect the listener from further mental distress. Another song that could be virtually any mediocre rock band seeking to crack the lucrative American market, 'Calling The Shots', is without any redeeming musical features. It's dull, uninventive, and, if it had a destiny, it would be as the play-out song in the credits of a rom-com 'straight to DVD' film of the same name. It's like getting a bonus track on a Yoko Ono album.

Back To Back

Personnel:
Francis Rossi
Richard Parfitt
Alan Lancaster
Andy Bown
Pete Kircher
Guest musician:
Bernie Frost: backing vocals
Produced by Status Quo
Engineered by Tim Summerhayes, and Steve Churchyard
Recorded at AIR Studios, Montserrat, and elsewhere.
Released on 3 December 1983
Highest chart position: 9
Weeks on chart: 22

Prior to the release of their sixteenth studio album, Phonogram unleashed the mother of all Quo compilations, *F.T.M.O*, on 13 November 1982. The title was an acronym of 'From The Makers Of…', the legend which had appeared on the rear of all Quo albums since *Piledriver;* the small, two colour representations of the album sleeves in chronological order.

Issued in a sturdy circular denim blue tin, the triple album included some of the major songs, mostly singles, from the Vertigo albums, together with a small number of their releases during the Pye era. The aural catnip for fans was a recording of a concert the band had given on 14 May 1982 for The Princes Trust, a charity supported by Prince Charles, which had the effect of turning Quo into a British Institution.

The gig was attended by the Prince, who was a huge fan of the band; one of his prized possessions being a framed copy of the *Hello!* sleeve signed by all four members in black marker pen. Only one part of that last sentence is true. What is true is that the profits from the gig were donated to The Prince's Trust, an organisation designed to help people under the age of 30 who were either unemployed or struggling with education. The show was (partially) broadcast live on television and in its entirety on Radio One.

Unusually for such a lavish box-set *F.T.M.O* rose to number four in the album charts as part of an eighteen-week stay. The studio tracks were:

'Pictures Of Matchstick Men'
'Ice In The Sun'
'Down The Dustpipe'
'In My Chair'
'Junior's Wailing'
'Mean Girl'

'Gerdundula'
'Paper Plane'
'Big Fat Mama'
'Roadhouse Blues'
'Break The Rules'
'Down Down'
'Bye Bye Johnny'
'Rain'
'Mystery Song'
'Blue For You'
'Is There A Better Way'
'Again And Again'
'Accident Prone'
'Wild Side Of Life'
'Living On An Island'
'What You're Proposing'
'Lies'
'Rock 'N Roll'
'Something 'Bout You Baby I Like'
'Dear John'

The live tracks were:

'Caroline'
'Roll Over Lay Down'
'Backwater'
'Little Lady'
'Don't Drive My Car'
'Whatever You Want'
'Hold You Back'
'Rocking All Over The World'
'Over The Edge'
'Don't Waste My Time'

The live version of 'Caroline' was released as a single on 30 October 1982 and reached number 13 in the charts.

The band took time off from each other following *1+9+8+2*, eventually reassembling on the Caribbean Island of Montserrat. This was the home of AIR Studios, which belonged to Beatles producer George Martin. Unsurprisingly the luxurious location, with its many distractions, did not result in much actual work being done. Additional recording sessions away from the island paradise enabled this set of duffers to be rescued from the debris in time to meet contractual obligations. It's hard to dislike *Back To Back* but it's well worth the effort, et cetera…

As appetisers for the release, 'Ol' Rag Blues' was issued as a single on 10 September 1983, swiftly followed by 'A Mess Of Blues' on 5 November. They got as high as nine and fifteen, respectively. Phonogram really milked *Back To Back* for all it was worth, which, in retrospect, wasn't very much at all; 'Marguerita Time' came out on 10 December, and was the bestseller of the album's four, yes four, singles reaching number three. 19 May 1984 saw the final escapce, 'Going Down Town Tonight', only get as far as number twenty. 'Back To Back' should have really been released on the 'Dead Horse' label for all the flogging that Phonogram gave it.

The album cover is as weak as its contents. Two heavy goods vehicles are parked next to each other on a road, one with the word 'Status' down one side, the other with 'Quo' on the opposite side, the eye being drawn down the lorries to a sunset at the vanishing point, a fine visual clue for the end of the band. The vehicles aren't even parked 'Back To Back'; the album should therefore have been called 'Side By Side', or, having listened to it, 'Slide and Slide'. The band logo and the album title are mirrored. On the rear of the sleeve, a live shot of Parfitt, Rossi and Lancaster is similarly reflected. Kircher's kit is visible, and Bown can just about be seen at the rear of the image. The sleeve design was credited to 'Andrew Prewitt and The Game', whilst Bob Elsdale provided the trucking image and Colin Johnston the rear view. It all looks cheap, unimaginative, and tired and is an entirely suitable metaphor for its contents.

The inter-band tensions were still rising, and two songs on *Back To Back* caused irreconcilable differences between Lancaster and Rossi, which spelt the end of the classic line-up. The first problem was a Lancaster/Lamb composition, 'Ol' Rag Blues'. Whilst both Rossi and Lancaster agreed the song should be a single, the bassist, not unreasonably, wanted to sing it. Rossi felt that Phonogram would only sanction a version featuring his unique, recognisable singing style, and, as a compromise, two versions were recorded. It was the Rossi version that prevailed, the record company making the purely commercial decision that the song would sell more if the perceived band vocalist sang it. Lancaster did not take this at all well.

But that was as nothing compared to the shitstorm of issues that 'Marguerita Time' unleashed. Phonogram insisted that this Rossi/Frost composition be released as a Christmas single. It's easy to see why; the song is a sunny sounding, country-style, lightweight, sing-a-long, party number with earworm melodies-a-plenty. But 'Marguerita Time' only served to divide fans even further into their partisan camps. The old guard Quo Army felt betrayed; what was this abomination? The newer fans, those who had found the band since 1977, liked it and sent it into the charts. Lancaster refused to have anything to do with its media promotion. By this point everybody had seemingly had enough of everyone else. In *Hello Quo!* Parfitt reflected on 'Marguerita Time':

It just had this impact on Alan where, you know, it was just a bit too much for him.

Lancaster offered up some fascinating new information:

> Yeah, it was a load of rubbish … I didn't want to record it, I didn't think it was right for the band, that's another story. It wasn't 'Marguerita Time' at all. If anything, it was 'Going Down Town Tonight' 'cos that wasn't a Status Quo song. It wasn't a Status Quo *performance*. Not one of us played on that, except Francis.

Rossi wrestled with the dilemmas of remaining within this unhappy unit over the 1983 Christmas holidays, eventually arriving at a decision that no one was pleased with, except him. He announced that he no longer wanted to perform live. This was reluctantly accepted by the others on the basis that one final and very lucrative tour would take place.

Officially the band was merely retiring from gigging, and there would be periodic new record releases. Unofficially they were sick of the sight of each other, and the greatest rift was between the two men who had started the group over twenty years ago. Lancaster, always the harder rocker, and Rossi, the melodic maestro with the penchant for country music, were now so far apart that any attempt at reconciliation would be a waste of time. The 'End Of The Road' tour, as it was semi-accurately dubbed, was in effect the end of the band. Although an agreement had been made to carry on recording, Lancaster returned to Australia, and the relationship between Parfitt and Rossi was severely strained at the time. Both guitarists decided to write, record, and release solo albums which only led to further problems.

Phonogram released *Live At The NEC* as a separate disc on 4 August 1984. This took the ten tracks previously available only on *F.T.M.O* and added 'Dirty Water' and 'Down Down' from the now two-year-old charity concert. The album's highest chart position was 83 during a three-week run. A 2017 deluxe reissue put the entire concert across two discs, the 'new' tracks being:

'Forty Five Hundred Times'
'Big Fat Mama'
'Roadhouse Blues'
'Rain'
'Bye Bye Johnny'

What '*Live At The NEC*' shows is, despite the often dubious production and song-writing qualities which had permeated the band's records since *Rocking…*, on stage they remained an incredibly tight, potent, and powerful force.

Spurred on by the success of *Twelve Gold Bars*, Phonogram released another compilation, with the imaginative title; *Twelve Gold Bars, Volume Two* on 23 November 1984. They were up all night working on that one. It featured:

'What You're Proposin''
'Lies'

'Something 'Bout You Baby I Like'
'Don't Drive My Car'
'Dear John'
'Rock N Roll'
'Ol' Rag Blues'
'Mess Of Blues'
'Marguerita Time'
'Going Down Town Tonight'
'The Wanderer'
'Caroline (Live at the NEC)'

Ironically the last time the now Frantic Three (plus one or two, depending upon how you did the maths), would perform together in the twentieth century would be in front of the largest audience they, or any other band, would ever play to.

Rossi and Parfitt had already been involved in the 1984 Band Aid charity single 'Do They Know It's Christmas'. Although the band was effectively over, Bob Geldof saw Quo's potential to open the subsequent Live Aid concert at Wembley on 13 July 1985 and used his powers of persuasion to great effect. Lancaster agreed to return from Australia for the performance. Quo played to 72,000 people in the stadium, with hundreds of millions watching on television. The songs featured were, inevitably, 'Rocking All Over The World', together with 'Caroline', and, strangely, 'Don't Waste My Time'. This reappearance fuelled hopes that a reformation was on the cards. It was not to be, at least not for nearly three decades.

'A Mess Of Blues' (Shuman/Pomus) Duration: 3.20 Chord Count: 5
This is a typically bouncy late-period Quo interpretation of the song originally recorded by Elvis Presley in 1960. Double-tracked Rossi vocals, with Bown honky-tonking away in the background over a regulation shuffle rhythm, provide the expected musical staples to this arrangement. Handclaps join in for the second section, ('Whoops, there goes a teardrop'), with a low register guitar providing a counter melody. On the plus side the overall recorded sound is crisper and better than the aural mess that was *1+8+9+2*.

There's a brief solo before another traipse through a further verse with the tried and trusted thrice-repeated final line leading into a false ending. Another simple, melodic solo takes the song into the fade. The seven-inch single was backed with 'Big Man', and the twelve-inch version added 'Young Pretender'. Now, there's a collection of magical tuneage for you. As opening tracks go, 'A Mess Of Blues' is dull and unremarkable, Standard Quo if you like, but it is also a clear marker for the rest of the album and what would become the future direction of the brand, a light-hearted, pop-rock-boogie band that entire generations of families could safely turn out to see.

'Ol' Rag Blues' (Lancaster) Duration: 2.49 Chord Count: 6

This starts promisingly with a strong guitar melody over a power-chord progression, but then the band soon slips back into comfortable commerciality they were wearing for 'A Mess Of Blues'. Lancaster's song is more muscular and has a greater energy than the opening track, despite the unnecessary presence of the keyboards.

At 1.57, there's a stronger section where Parfitt takes over the vocals and Quo actually start to sound slightly like the rock band they used to be. This short, powerful mood is quickly dissipated by a return to the main style and substance of the song. There's a brief, unspectacular solo before the coda section, where the music slows dramatically into stylish end with a nice piano arpeggio to round things off. The seven inch single was backed with 'Stay The Night', with the twelve-inch version featuring 'Whatever You Want', taken from the Princes Trust Concert.

The (rejected) version with Lancaster on vocals is not markedly different to the familiar recording, but hearing the bassist's voice on his own song makes a refreshing change to the constant Rossi-ness, which dominates *Back To Back*. Lyrically Lancaster's song is directed at the band themselves; 'What you gonna do with those faded blues you wear? What you gonna do with those ol' rag blues?', as opposed to the 'Blues as melancholy' referenced in the opening track.

'Can't Be Done' (Rossi/Frost) Duration: 3.03 Chord Count: 11

A gritty guitar opening leads quickly into the by-now-familiar musical territory. What sounds encouraging, to begin with, inevitably becomes a further overly commercial, too heavily arranged song to be effective. There's an unexpected twist underneath the title lyric where a bar of 3/4 time leads into three bars of 5/4 to give the track an effective syncopated feel. After the second verse, a bridge section appears with added instrumentation. Another verse and a repeat of the bridge leads into a section where a lot of instruments compete for attention behind Rossi's solo. After a couple of neat false endings, the song goes into a fade. It's okay, but that's all it is. 'Can't Be Done' was the B-side to 'The Wanderer'.

'Too Close To The Ground' (Parfitt/Bown) Duration: 3.41 Chord Count: 12

This is a slow, dreary blues which sounds like it has pretensions of being a follow-up to 'Blue For You'. The musical equivalent of watching a horse trying to eat its food with a fork held in its hooves. 'Too Close To The Ground' is quickly spoilt by some typical early Eighties keyboards and production touches which banish it to much needed obscurity in the Quo Canon. The second verse has some unwelcome violin synthesizer tones clogging up the mix, and when the solo arrives, it's spoilt by heavily reverbed percussion. The dynamic tension increases to an effective break, where the vocals and a subdued backing return.

Keyboards continue to add unnecessary levels of chewy aural stodge to what could have been an effective number if less had been going on for most of the time. 'Too Close To The Ground' was the B side to 'Going Down Town Tonight', and what a joy that must have been to purchase.

'No Contract' (Parfitt/Bown) Duration: 3.39 Chord Count: 5

What might be a reasonable if pedestrian rocker is undermined by the horrible gated and reverbed drum sound, and a swamping of the mix with the keyboards. Somewhere in the middle of all this mess is a decent guitar riff that has been listening to 'All Night Long' by Rainbow (1979), but, as before, there's just *so much* going on instrumentally, and this undermines the song. It sounds more like an off-cut from the nascent AOR Hair Metal scene which was gaining in popularity at the time than an actual Quo song.

Parfitt is back to barking at the microphone, and there's an excellent use of a flanger effect (1.06) just prior to the title words, but the tempo feels flaccid and the track itself lacks enthusiasm. As a showcase for the popular production sounds and techniques of the time, 'No Contract' is first class. As a side closing song on a Quo album, it's the sound of the bottom of the barrel being scraped. What is a distinctly under-par offering from the usually reliable Parfitt becomes a better than average song for this album, which tells you all you need to know about *Back To Back*.

'Win Or Lose' (Rossi/Frost) Duration: 2.34 Chord Count: 5

This is, of course, a Rossi and Frost composition. Up tempo, major key, and cheerfully commercial, it is very similar to any number of other undistinguished tracks dating back to the Pip Williams era ('Can't Give You More', 'Run To Mummy' *et al*). There's a strong country rock feel to 'Win Or Lose', and, weirdly, Rossi's guitar fills sound more like a chirpy synthesizer than a biting Telecaster. In the end, it's just another Quo song from the 1980s; there would be a *lot* more like this over the ensuing decades; formulaic, predictable, and unrewarding.

'Marguerita Time' (Rossi/Frost) Duration: 3.26 Chord Count: 6

However, *all* the preceding tracks are preferable to this piece of utter garbage. This is the third contender for the 'Triumvirate of Tripe' that started with 'Someone Show Me Home' and begat 'Rock 'N Roll'. The back-story to the song is that Marguerita had become Rossi's recent (excessive) tipple of choice and, like anything taken to excess, sickness ensues. Here it sets in as soon we reach the end of the introduction.

As a commercial light country song, it is almost without compare. As a single by one of the leading rock bands of the day, it's a complete disgrace, and a total refutation of the band's hard-earned reputation. There's a cheery melodic introduction, an easy listening, foot-tapping rhythm, and very hummable melodies set against the more than usually nonsensical lyrics. Somewhere in the mix is a Quo guitar rhythm, but twee keyboards, forward sounding drums and double-tracked vocals manage quickly to suffocate any life out of the composition. In summary, it starts, it continues and then it ends. The last bit is the best bit.

'Your Kind Of Love' (Lancaster/Skinner) Duration: 3.21 Chord Count: 6

Lancaster sings this lame pop number. This is another weak composition that belongs halfway through the weak soundtrack album to a glossy American teen rom-com, without being strong enough to have earned a place in the actual film itself. After a semi-interesting guitar opening, a dull throbbing rhythm takes hold and, like an out of condition Boa Constrictor, just can't be bothered to let go. 'Your Kind Of Love' chugs away with lyrical clichés and production touches abounding. At its core, this is a *very* average song indeed. There's an alarming lack of distinguishing features here, and the track quickly becomes aural wallpaper. This is the sound of a band going through the motions, with an absence of creativity or integrity to the music they are making.

'Stay The Night' (Rossi/Frost/Miller) Duration: 3.00 Chord Count: 7

An introduction that sounds like The Eagles in their latter-day rock mode soon adopts a solid rock backing until the verse arrives. Oh. Dear. God. 'Stay The Night' quickly becomes a routine pop-rock song that manages to bore by the bar. All the problems which have plagued *Back To Back* are present and correct, with Bown's keyboard intrusions sounding like a cheap Bontempi organ. If you look closely enough, you can now see the ground beneath the barrel.

'Going Down Town Tonight' (Johnson) Duration: 3.36 Chord Count: 5

It doesn't get any better; it just doesn't. More chirruping keyboards and a poppy tempo are the weak spines to this inane, irritating little bopper. Kircher has now fully evolved into a drum machine, and whilst the chorus has some slight melodic interest, the overall effect is of a band past caring what their audience thinks of them. A re-recorded version of 'Going Down Town Tonight' was the last single to be released from the album. Surprisingly, this re-polished turd remains a turd.

And that's it; well done, you've made it to the end of *Back To Back*, and may be wondering why you bothered in the first place. The album is the absolute nadir of the band's output, and it's understandable that the combination of increasing personality clashes, musical differences, drink, drugs, and possible outright exhaustion caused the band to effectively knock themselves on the head.

Non-Album Track

'The Wanderer' (Maresca) Duration: 3.30 Chord Count: 5

This was the final song released as a single by this line up of the band and reached number seven in the charts. It's a boisterous reinterpretation of the song first performed by Dion (of Dion and The Belmonts fame) on his 1961 album *Runaround Sue*.

Aside from some typically chunky guitars, Quo's version doesn't stray too far away from the original. Again it's a Rossi fronted number, although Parfitt takes over the vocals for the more powerful middle eight-bar section. Bown's ivories are prominent in the mix, and the whole tune has a good time rock'n'roll feel to it. 'The Wanderer' was the band's farewell to their fans, along with 'The End Of The Road Tour'. Not so much a 'farewell', more a 'sod off', then.

Again, and Again, and Again, and Again, and Again, and Again, and Again...

The genesis for the 'new' Quo was in the solo albums Rossi and Parfitt had been working on while the original band fell apart. Rossi had recorded *Flying Debris* with Bernie Frost, and Parfitt had hired Pip Williams to produce and play on his own project, *Recorded Delivery*. Williams recommended a rhythm section he had worked with in the past. This consisted of bassist John 'Rhino' Edwards (so-called as it was apparently unwise to stand downwind of him), and Jeff Rich, who looked like he could easily fit at least 25 Maltesers in his hamster-like jowls whilst hitting things with sticks.

After their appearance at 'Live Aid', Quo were suddenly thrust back into the limelight whilst simultaneously ceasing to exist. Phonogram wanted a new album, and the label would not agree to the release of either *Flying Debris* or *Recorded Delivery* as alternatives. Phonogram was resolute in their requirement; as long as Quo consisted of at least Rossi and Parfitt, then a band-branded album could be released.

Rossi agreed reluctantly, but only on the proviso that the project wouldn't involve Lancaster. Upon hearing the news, the bassist, ever the fighter, took out an injunction forbidding Quo to exist without him being a part of it. Eventually, and with much bad blood being spilled between the warring parties, an out of court settlement was reached. With Kircher being semi-retired and overlooked, Parfitt suggested that Rossi, Bown, and he work with Edwards and Rich. The new rhythm section officially joined the existing trio in March 1986.

Thus Status Quo was re-launched to a waiting world, and those hoping for a return to the 'glory days' would, yet again, be disappointed. The band had been drifting away from their hard rock roots since 1977 and were now about to enter their most commercially successful period, in gigs if not chart-topping album sales. For the long-term fans, the boat containing their musical integrity had sailed many moons ago. The absence of Lancaster further cemented the fact that a heavy rock bias would not be a feature of their future. This incarnation would be the pop-boogie Quo, an audio image Rossi had been cultivating for the last few years and one which would endure, with chart success and gig longevity, to a fan-base spanning generations of families.

Rossi and Parfitt were now seen as being 'the band', and frequent media and promotional appearances emphasised the fact that the pair was, to all intents and purposes, Status Quo. Yes, there'd also be the tall thin one playing the bass, the older tall, thin one on keyboards and sometimes guitar, and some other guy of indeterminate personality building sheds at the back of the stage, but Quo was now fundamentally a duo with additional musicians. Despite the constant presence of Bown (as of 2021, the second longest-serving member of the band), and Edwards, who continues as bassist to this day, the public's perception was that the most important elements remained the two guitarists. Quo was Rossi and Parfitt and whoever else was with them at the time.

Since the demise of the Frantic Four, Status Quo have made a further seventeen studio albums. Whilst a detailed review of this output is not a part of this book's remit, I feel it appropriate to at least offer brief overviews of their substantial portfolio over the past 35 years. Brace yourselves…

In The Army Now
Released on 29 August 1986
Highest chart position: 7

In The Army Now is a glossy, poppy, lightweight and, at times, extremely painful affair. Produced by Pip Williams, and Dave Edmunds, Quo's seventeenth is, of course, disappointing. Stand-out tracks are few and far between, although 'End Of The Line' and 'Red Sky' are reasonable efforts. Only reasonable, mind you, not actually *good*. 'Rollin' Home' (no relation), 'Save Me', and 'Dreaming' are formulaic and hugely predictable, whilst 'Calling', 'In Your Eyes', and 'Overdose' are weak, uninspiring space fillers. 'Invitation' is a beyond-awful soft country song, and 'Speechless' is a horrible sounding example of family-friendly pop that is little short of disgraceful for a supposed rock band.

The title track single, written by the Dutch duo Bolland and Bolland, is fine but, Rossi's voice aside, the band really could be any mid-1980s 'rock' group. Contrary to rumours which circulated at the time, the voice shouting, 'Stand up and fight!' at 2.09 is not Alan Lancaster. Parfitt later commented;

The title song was great, but it had too many fillers.

Ain't Complaining
Released on 13 June 1988
Highest chart position: 12

The follow up didn't fare as well commercially as *In The Army Now,* despite, or perhaps because of, Pip Williams' retention as producer. *Ain't Complaining* was the first Quo album not to hit the top ten since *Dog Of Two Head*, and it's easy to see why. Even more reliant on shiny keyboards and undemanding pop-rock compositions, this underwhelming collection is mainly a display of late 1980s production techniques.

The title track sets the low bar for what follows. 'Everytime I Think Of You', and 'One For The Money' give us a new definition of 'average', whilst 'Another Shipwreck' wants to be a glossy, American chart hit. Two ballads ('I Know You're Leaving' and 'Who Gets The Love?') are pretty enough in the stylistic sound mould of the era. 'The Loving Game' is a semi-decent rocker struggling to get out of its sonic straitjacket, whilst 'Cross That Bridge' and 'Cream Of The Crop' try to be heavy but only manage to sound clichéd. The execrable 'Burning Bridges' is probably the album's lowest point, with its instrumental melody being almost a complete lift from the traditional tune 'Darby Kelly'. Parfitt offered up the following opinion:

> The music was too polite. There was no weight behind what we were doing. The edge had gone; we weren't real anymore.

Rick, mate, you hadn't been 'real' for years before this abomination appeared...

Perfect Remedy
Released on 17 November 1989
Highest chart position: 49

The following year's offering dialled down the over-production. Another Pip Williams project, *Perfect Remedy* was recorded at Nassau in the Bahamas. Again, the paucity of decent songs and possibly fan dissatisfaction with the band's drift in musical direction meant a lowly chart showing. Of its twelve tracks, only 'The Power Of Rock' managed to stand out above a very mediocre crowd, whilst 'Little Dreamer', 'Not At All', and the title track feel underpowered and utterly predictable. 'Heart On Hold', 'Address Book', 'Tommy's In Love', and '1000 Years' are both terrible and embarrassing. None of the remaining songs are worth the printer ink.

Rock 'Til You Drop
Released on 24 September 1991
Highest chart position: 10

Rossi acted as producer for the band's last album for Phonogram. *Rock 'Til You Drop*, whilst still brightly commercial and, at times, tellingly formulaic, contained some stronger material, with a much better-recorded sound. Sixteen tracks long, this was a studio double album, and had it been pruned back would have been a more involving affair.

'Like A Zombie', 'One Man Band', and 'No Problems' raised some pulses, whilst on the softer side, the reflective title track and 'Warning Shot' are curiously affecting. 'Good Sign' has an excellent riff and groove before Parfitt goes into barking mode, and 'Nothing Comes Easy' features some excellent guitar interplay. Strangely, the band decided, unwisely, to reinterpret 'Forty Five Hundred Times' and 'Can't Give You More', along with three other ill-advised cover versions; 'Let's Work Together' (Canned Heat), 'Bring It On Home' (Sam Cooke), and 'The Price Of Love' (The Everly Brothers). Why? Still don't know.

Thirsty Work
Released on 27 August 1994
Highest chart position: 13

Not so much thirsty work as downright hard work to listen to, the next album was another Rossi production and the band's first for their new label, Polydor. *Thirsty Work* is, again, a sixteen-track opus. The opening song, 'Goin' Nowhere', pretty much sums things up, and 'Point Of No Return' seemed prophetic in retrospect. Overall *Thirsty Work* is, yet again, nothing special, with a light, poppy sound and more forgettable material. Diverse and desperately disappointing, step forward the main offenders; 'Sail Away', Like It Or Not', 'Lover Of The Human Race', and 'Sherri Don't Fail Me Now'. Only the quite magnificent 'Ciao Ciao', and, to a lesser degree, 'I Didn't Mean It' and 'Rude Awakening Time' serve as reminders that Quo still had the potential to deliver the goods. When they could be bothered.

Don't Stop: The 30th Anniversary Album
Released on 5 February 1996
Highest chart position: 2

Pip Williams oversaw this embarrassing disaster. Under management pressure to produce 'product', a deeply moronic, all-cover collection was cobbled together as the poorest definition yet of the word 'celebration'. The 'modern day' Quo treatment is administered, anaesthetic-like, to genuine classic songs by The Beach Boys, The Beatles, Fleetwood Mac, Creedence Clearwater Revival and Steeleye Span, amongst others.

It is an awful listening experience, almost beyond description. More accurately titled 'Please Stop', this was, for many of the old guard, too much to take. In their eyes, the band had finally turned into the poor punch line to their own bad joke and completely destroyed all vestiges of any remaining credibility.

Under The Influence
Released on 31 March 1999
Highest chart position: 26

Three years later, Quo somehow managed to turn in a more respectable collection, partly due to Parfitt's return to composing credits (having been an absentee since *Rock 'Til You Drop*) and the introduction of Mike Paxman's more rock-centric production style.

'Twenty Wild Horses', 'Shine On', 'Keep 'Em Coming' and 'Makin' Waves' all have decent pop-rock credentials, but there are, inevitably, disappointments including 'Little White Lies', 'Little Me And You' and 'Blessed Are The Meek'. Bizarrely Buddy Holly's 'Not Fade Away' received an unnecessary country rock workout. *Under The Influence* was the last album to feature songs co-written by Rossi and Frost. The guitarist would soon join forces once again with Bob Young.

Famous In The Last Century
Released on 5 April 2000
Highest chart position: 19

The band's manager at the time, David Walker, must take responsibility for this truly terrible, reputation desecrating record. The fact that it charted at all proves that some people will buy anything if it's got the words 'Status' and 'Quo' on it. The 'Big Idea' was to 'celebrate the Millennium' (translation; 'extract more money from a willing and pliant fan base') by releasing an album of twenty of the band's 'favourite songs' from the twentieth century. What a work of towering genius.

The emphasis was supposed to be on the early years of rock'n'roll, although, strangely, Seventies rock compadres Lynyrd Skynyrd, Steve Miller, and Ian Hunter (of Mott The Hoople fame) also got the nod. Jeff Rich left the band after recording this album. I don't blame him.

Heavy Traffic
Released on 15 September 2002
Highest chart position: 15

Again produced by Mike Paxman and the first release to feature new drummer Matt Letley, this is a rockier collection, both in sound and song writing. A more cohesive album than either *Under The Influence* or *Thirsty Work*, *Heavy Traffic* bore the fruits of Rossi and Young writing together again. The album sold well, but, again, failed to contain any outstanding tracks. 'Blues And Rhythm', 'All Stand Up', 'Solid Gold', and 'Do It Again' displayed some worthwhile muscle. 'Green' is an interesting acoustic-based groover, but other songs, including 'Jam Side Down' and the peculiarly titled 'Diggin' Burt Bacharach', lack inspiration and sound insipid.

Riffs
Released on 23 December 2003
Highest chart position: 44

Another Paxman production, another confusing compilation, this release contained ten covers of other artist's songs and five of their own; 'Caroline', 'Junior's Wailing', 'Down The Dustpipe', 'Whatever You Want', and 'Rocking All Over The World'. Why? Just why? The world didn't need this, and a diminishing proportion of the record-buying public wanted a copy, resulting in a justifiably low chart score.

The Party Ain't Over Yet
Released on 19 September 2005
Highest chart position: 18

The title track is a rocked-up cover of a country song, and country rock dominates much of the album. 'Belavista Man', 'Goodbye Baby', 'Kick Me When I'm Down', and the title track provide a degree of weight, whilst 'Familiar Blues', 'The Bubble', and 'This Is Me', among others, deliver the expected levels of disappointment. In the end, *The Party Ain't Over Yet* is yet another commercially aware, memory-dodging collection. Paxman was retained as producer, but the rule regarding turd polishing remains resolutely relevant.

In Search Of The Fourth Chord
Released on 17 September 2007
Highest chart position: 15

This album, with its cartoon-esque Indiana Jones theme, marked the return of Pip Williams as producer. Oh. Deep joy. With tongues firmly lodged in cheek, this collection is musically diverse and emotionally dispiriting in equal measure. *In Search Of The Fourth Chord* suggests that the band's heart just isn't in it anymore. 'Gravy Train', 'You're The One For Me', 'Hold Me', and 'Bad News' display some meaningful power, but the other songs drift past the ears without bothering either heart or mind. 'Pennsylvania Blues Tonight', 'Figure Of Eight', the Lennon-esque 'Tongue Tied', and 'Electric Arena' are particularly poor. The bar sinks ever lower…

Quid Pro Quo
Released on 27 May 2010
Highest chart position: 10

Produced jointly by Rossi and Paxman, *Quid Pro Quo* is a return to some sort of rocking form. 'Two Way Traffic' is a fine, driving opener, whilst 'Can't See For Looking', 'Movin' On', and 'Leave A Light On' are reasonably strong amongst the expected commercial pop-rock fare paraded here. Elsewhere Parfitt's terrible, derivative 'Let's Rock' is wall-to-wall lyrical clichés set to utterly predictable music, and 'Any Way You Like It' is weak country pop. The album included a re-recorded version of *In The Army Now*, for some reason.

Bula Quo!
Released on 10 June 2013
Highest chart position: 10

This double soundtrack album to the film of the same name was the last to feature drummer Matt Letley. Produced by Rossi, Parfitt, and Paxman, *Bula Quo!*, featured nine new songs, together with new versions of 'Living On An Island' and 'Rocking All Over The World', and the unremarkable 'Frozen Hero' and 'Reality Cheque', from *Quid Pro Quo*. Why? Don't care. The album included live performances of six other previously released songs, spanning the band's career from 'Pictures Of Matchstick Men' to 'Beginning Of The End'.

Aqoustic: Stripped Bare

Released on 17 November 2014
Highest chart position: 5

Proving the adage that a good song will translate into a different musical genre, new life was breathed into familiar tracks with refreshing results. The first acoustic greatest hits collection also introduced the band's fifth drummer, Leon Cave, with additional musicians on violins, viola, cello, and accordion reimagining an almost exclusively 'Frantic Four' era set-list. The cover image of a naked Rossi and Parfitt 'protected' by their acoustic guitars showed the public that this was to be a Quo album like no other, and so it proved to be.

Aquostic II: That's A Fact

Released on 21 October 2016
Highest chart position: 7

If a thing is worth doing once, etc, etc. This was the inevitable follow-up to the band's well regarded acoustic reboot. *Aquostic II: That's A Fact* has a greater emphasis on the post 'Frantic Four' period and included a couple of brand new songs; 'One For The Road' and 'One Of Everything'.

Backbone

Released on 6 September 2019
Highest chart position: 6

By the time of 'Backbone's release, Parfitt had been dead for three years. In effect, Quo was now The Francis Rossi Group. But the band is the brand, and so 2019 saw another album from Status Quo, fronted by the only original member. Parfitt's replacement, Richie Malone, complete with requisite white Telecaster, took over rhythm guitar duties. Stand out tracks include 'Cut Me Some Slack', Better Take Care', and 'Get Out Of My Head' in what is, at times, a surprisingly rocking collection.

In the sleeve notes to *Backbone*, the band's 33rd studio album, Rossi summarised the band's position:

Backbone is a real statement of where the band is right now, and I'm really pleased with it, and knocked out about how everyone played and contributed. There's a sense of unity about the whole collection and about the band itself. This album is about change as well as unity; now that Richie (Malone) has settled in to being a full member of the band and we have performed 130 shows. This is the sound of Quo in 2019. Whilst to us it sounds fresh and vital, we'll never lose that signature Quo sound.

Perhaps Rossi should have added the word 'again'.

The Frantic Four Reformation

Time's capacity to heal old wounds was demonstrated when, at Coghlan's suggestion, Lancaster went to see a Quo show in Australia, where he later met up with Rossi. This was later described by Bob Young in 2013:

When Francis and Alan got together in Sydney a couple of years ago, from that meeting, of Alan going over to the hotel and having coffee with Francis, seeing Richard and all that, all the bullshit of all those years seemed to wash away. Everyone was talking to each other again, Francis and Alan on Skype two or three times a week for those last couple of years as well. As far as trying to remember when it was mooted that they were all going to get back together again, it really was probably a year ago. Once the thing started formulating on the ideas, then it was, you know, it could be a reality, but don't let's put too many shows on, don't let's make them too big, let's just basically test the water. And then when those first five shows sold out in, whatever it was, minutes, and the other four were put in, it was suddenly a reality. So then, it was, well we've got an audience, now what we've got to do is put a set together. And there are not really many hit singles in there, and yet there are a lot of big Quo songs because a lot of the big Quo songs were not hit singles, just great album tracks.

All nine dates of the tour (two in Manchester, two in Glasgow, two in Wolverhampton, and three in London) were recorded and released. I went to the Manchester gig at the O2 Apollo on Tuesday, 12 March 2013. Although Lancaster was battling ill-health and Parfitt a poorly advised haircut, it was a magnificent night, both for music and nostalgia. The band decided to use their 1976 album *Live* as a set-list template but also made space for some surprising inclusions:

'Junior's Wailing'
'Backwater'
'Just Take Me'
'Is There A Better Way'
'In My Chair'
'Blue Eyed Lady'
'Little Lady'
'Most Of The Time'
'(April), Spring, Summer and Wednesdays'
'Railroad'
'Oh Baby'
'Forty Five Hundred Times'
'Rain'
'Big Fat Mama'
'Down Down'
'Roadhouse Blues'

'Don't Waste My Time'
'Bye Bye Johnny'

And so it came to pass in the following year that the show went on back on the road again, this time under the imaginative banner of 'BACK 2 SQ.1' with sixteen gigs across Europe in March 2014, finishing off in Dublin on 12 April. This concert was recorded and released as *The Frantic Four's Final Fling*. The set list was almost identical; 'Gotta Go Home' was included in edited form, and 'Caroline' replaced 'Don't Waste My Time'. Speaking in 2015, Parfitt commented:

> The line-up now, which changed in the mid-1980s, is, in fact, a much better band, musically. It has a certain kind of magic about it, but it's not the Frantic Four! That was just something very, very special that you can never find, because it was magic. And you can't create that.

Beyond the highly lucrative nature of the brief reformation, what was most important was that the original band parted on good terms. The 'other' Quo then took up where they had left off.

However, Parfitt's rock'n'roll lifestyle finally caught up with him on Christmas Eve 2016. He died of a sepsis infection in hospital near his home in Marbella, Spain. Parfitt was the epitome of the Seventies rock and roll star; he looked the part, and most definitely lived it. He had faced health issues before, including a quadruple heart bypass in 1997, a throat cancer scare in 2005, and heart attacks in 2011 and 2014. These, and an awareness of the advance of time, led to the *Aquostic* albums and the announcement of a 'Last Of The Electrics' Tour in 2016. Unfortunately, Parfitt was not well enough to participate following a further heart attack in 2016, but he gave his approval to his stand in, Irish guitarist Richie Malone, as he retired from the band.

On 26th September 2021 Alan Charles Lancaster died at the age of 72. Rossi subsequently issued a statement to the media

> I am so sorry to hear of Alan's passing. We were friends and colleagues for many years and achieved fantastic success together as the Frantic Four alongside Rick Parfitt and John Coghlan. Alan was an integral part of the sound and the enormous success of Status Quo during the 60s and 70s. Although it is well documented that we were estranged in recent years, I will always have very fond memories of our early days together and my condolences go to Dayle (Lancaster's wife) and Alan's family.

Quo's current manager, Simon Porter, stated

> This is such sad news and my sincere condolences go out to Dayle and the family It was an absolute pleasure to be able to reunite the original line-up for

two sell-out tours in 2013/2014 and to give Status Quo Frantic Four fans a final legacy and such a lasting memory. Although Alan was not in the best of health even then, he got through the tours with determination and grit and was a pleasure to work with

Lancaster suffered from multiple sclerosis, and died at his home in Sydney, Australia, surrounded by his family. Known to the legions of Quo fans as 'Nuff', an approximate translation from the French for 'little pig', which – whilst insulting – was clearly something that the bassist was happy to be associated with.

Status Quo's total worldwide record sales exceed 118,000,000 units. They have released over 100 singles, made 106 appearances on *Top Of The Pops*, and spent over 415 weeks (seven and a half years in old money) in the singles charts. Their album chart success is eclipsed only by The Rolling Stones. Quo's legendary gigging schedule means they have played an estimated 6000 plus shows to a total audience in excess of 25,000,000 people. This also translates into travelling approximately 4,000,000 miles and spending over 23 years away from home.

Rossi and Parfitt were awarded OBEs (Orders of the British Empire) for their services to music and substantial charity work. The band entered the *Guinness Book Of Records* when they played four shows in Britain (Sheffield, Glasgow, Birmingham, and Wembley in London) in eleven hours and eleven minutes. In 1991 the band were presented with the most prestigious award in British music, the 'Outstanding Contribution To The British Music Industry'. This was followed in the same year when HSH Prince Albert of Monaco gave them the 'Outstanding Contribution To The Rock Industry' award at the World Music Awards in Monte Carlo.

Whilst all these facts and figures are impressive, you are probably more concerned with the results of the chord survey announced at the start of this book. Does the lame old cliché stand up to forensic examination? Time for a final chapter…

The End Of This Road...

This book has reviewed 150 songs, from 'Spinning Wheel Blues', the first track on *Ma Kelly's Greasy Spoon* in 1970, to 1984's final single 'The Wanderer'. Some have been magnificent, most have been good, some have failed spectacularly and a few represent Quo's entries into a Nuremburg Trials-style litany of Crimes Against Rock Music. In the first chapter, I posed four vital questions:

1. How many songs by the 'Frantic Four' actually consist of just three chords?
2. What is the average number of chords per song?
3. Which song has the highest total?
4. Which song has the lowest total?

It is beyond dispute that this is important academic musical research, and definitely not a desperate attempt to fill in the hours by a middle-aged man with a Telecaster and too much time on his hands during a pandemic. Anyway, the results are now in...

How many songs by the 'Frantic Four' actually consist of just three chords?

Only 12 out of 150. Yes, I was surprised too. Less than 10%, then.

What is the average number of chords per song?

6.67, although it's tricky to have two-thirds of a chord. That's statistics for you. So, rounding up a more than acceptable seven, then.

Which song has the highest total?

'I Want The World To Know', with 15. Honourable mentions go to 'Living On An Island' and 'Whatever You Want' with 14 each.

Which song has the lowest total?

Pick any one from the 'Three Chord Twelve'; 'Paper Plane' is as good a starting and finishing point as any other.

Diving even deeper into this ground-breaking study, Quo's output can be further categorised thus:

3 chord songs:............ 12
4 chord songs: 17
5 chord songs: 27
6 chord songs: 27
7 chord songs: 15
8 chord songs: 22

9 chord songs: 10
10 chord songs: 7
11 chord songs: 5
12 chord songs: 4
13 chord songs: 1
14 chord songs: 2
15 chord songs: 1

So a more accurate insult would be 'Status Quo? They're just six and/or seven chord wonders'. Factually accurate, but it doesn't roll off the tongue quite so easily.

The final thoughts on the subject should surely go to Andy Bown, who has been waiting patiently at the back with his hand up for most of this book, and since the start of the *Hello Quo!* DVD. Andy...

It's not three chords, of course. Some of them are as many as five chords, and on Leap Years we put a minor in.

So, there you have it, straight from the horse's mouth, as it were. No offence.

I may be putting the anal into analysis here, but looking at the band's output through the prism of writing combinations, the most prolific song writing partnerships have been:

Rossi and Young: 32
Rossi and Frost: 21
Lancaster: 19
Cover versions: 13
Parfitt and Bown: 11
Lancaster and Parfitt: . 8
Rossi and Parfitt: 7
Parfitt: 6
Entire band: 5
Parfitt and Young: 3
Rossi and Lancaster: .. 3
Lancaster and Green: . 3
Lancaster and Lamb: . 3
Outside writers: .... °2

In addition, there are thirteen other individual songs with combinations of Parfitt, Lancaster, Frost, Lynton, Bown, Young, and Rossi. (Look, I'm still in lockdown here, it's either this or trying to predict how many times Richard Osman will say 'Nicely done' on tonight's edition of *House Of Games*).

Over the fourteen-year scope of this book, Status Quo produced some of the best rock music of the Seventies. There are numerous 'Greatest Hits' collections available, and they all tend to tread the same familiar, chart-topping ground. As an alternative, I suggest the following, which takes a song from each album to demonstrate that there is more, so much more, to the band beyond being 'three (or six and two-thirds of a chord) wonders'.

Ma Kelly's Greasy Spoon: '(April), Spring Summer, and Wednesdays'
Dog Of Two Head: 'Gerdundula'
Piledriver: 'Unspoken Words'
Hello!: 'And It's Better Now'
Quo: 'Lonely Man'
On The Level: 'Where I Am'
Blue For You: 'That's A Fact'
Rocking All Over The World: 'Who Am I?'
If You Can't Stand The Heat…: 'Long Legged Linda'
Whatever You Want: 'Living On An Island'
Just Supposin…: 'Over The Edge'
Never Too Late: 'Take Me Away'
1+9+8+2: 'I Want The World To Know'
Back To Back: 'Ol Rag Blues'

Burn those songs onto a CD and give it to someone who you think needs help with their understanding of just how good a band Quo were when they were in their prime. Think of it as an alternative list of great Quo songs, a kind of 'Best Of, for sceptics'. Or just buy *Blue For You* and have done with it!

'Ooh, I like this; who is it?'
'Status Quo'
'Really? It's good, isn't it?'

Yes. It really is.

On Track series

Tori Amos – Lisa Torem 978-1-78952-142-9

Asia – Peter Braidis 978-1-78952-099-6

Barclay James Harvest – Keith and Monica Domone 978-1-78952-067-5

The Beatles – Andrew Wild 978-1-78952-009-5

The Beatles Solo 1969-1980 – Andrew Wild 978-1-78952-030-9

Blue Oyster Cult – Jacob Holm-Lupo 978-1-78952-007-1

Marc Bolan and T.Rex – Peter Gallagher 978-1-78952-124-5

Kate Bush – Bill Thomas 978-1-78952-097-2

Camel – Hamish Kuzminski 978-1-78952-040-8

Caravan – Andy Boot 978-1-78952-127-6

Eric Clapton Solo – Andrew Wild 978-1-78952-141-2

The Clash – Nick Assirati 978-1-78952-077-4

Crosby, Stills and Nash – Andrew Wild 978-1-78952-039-2

The Damned – Morgan Brown 978-1-78952-136-8

Deep Purple and Rainbow 1968-79 – Steve Pilkington 978-1-78952-002-6

Dire Straits – Andrew Wild 978-1-78952-044-6

The Doors – Tony Thompson 978-1-78952-137-5

Dream Theater – Jordan Blum 978-1-78952-050-7

Elvis Costello and The Attractions – Georg Purvis 978-1-78952-129-0

Emerson Lake and Palmer – Mike Goode 978-1-78952-000-2

Fairport Convention – Kevan Furbank 978-1-78952-051-4

Peter Gabriel – Graeme Scarfe 978-1-78952-138-2

Genesis – Stuart MacFarlane 978-1-78952-005-7

Gentle Giant – Gary Steel 978-1-78952-058-3

Gong – Kevan Furbank 978-1-78952-082-8

Hawkwind – Duncan Harris 978-1-78952-052-1

Roy Harper – Opher Goodwin 978-1-78952-130-6

Iron Maiden – Steve Pilkington 978-1-78952-061-3

Jethro Tull – Jordan Blum 978-1-78952-016-3

Elton John in the 1970s – Peter Kearns 978-1-78952-034-7

Gong – Kevan Furbank 978-1-78952-082-8

The Incredible String Band – Tim Moon 978-1-78952-107-8

Iron Maiden – Steve Pilkington 978-1-78952-061-3

Judas Priest – John Tucker 978-1-78952-018-7

Kansas – Kevin Cummings 978-1-78952-057-6

Level 42 – Matt Philips 978-1-78952-102-3

Aimee Mann – Jez Rowden 978-1-78952-036-1

Joni Mitchell – Peter Kearns 978-1-78952-081-1

The Moody Blues – Geoffrey Feakes 978-1-78952-042-2

Mike Oldfield – Ryan Yard 978-1-78952-060-6

Tom Petty – Richard James 978-1-78952-128-3

Queen – Andrew Wild 978-1-78952-003-3

Renaissance – David Detmer 978-1-78952-062-0

The Rolling Stones 1963-80 – Steve Pilkington 978-1-78952-017-0
Steely Dan – Jez Rowden 978-1-78952-043-9
Steve Hackett – Geoffrey Feakes 978-1-78952-098-9
Thin Lizzy – Graeme Stroud 978-1-78952-064-4
Toto – Jacob Holm-Lupo 978-1-78952-019-4
U2 – Eoghan Lyng 978-1-78952-078-1
UFO – Richard James 978-1-78952-073-6
The Who – Geoffrey Feakes 978-1-78952-076-7
Roy Wood and the Move – James R Turner 978-1-78952-008-8
Van Der Graaf Generator – Dan Coffey 978-1-78952-031-6
Yes – Stephen Lambe 978-1-78952-001-9
Frank Zappa 1966 to 1979 – Eric Benac 978-1-78952-033-0
10CC – Peter Kearns 978-1-78952-054-5

Decades Series
Alice Cooper in the 1970s – Chris Sutton 978-1-78952-104-7
Curved Air in the 1970s – Laura Shenton 978-1-78952-069-9
Fleetwood Mac in the 1970s – Andrew Wild 978-1-78952-105-4
Focus in the 1970s – Stephen Lambe 978-1-78952-079-8
Marillion in the 1980s – Nathaniel Webb 978-1-78952-065-1
Pink Floyd In The 1970s – Georg Purvis 978-1-78952-072-9
The Sweet in the 1970s – Darren Johnson 978-1-78952-139-9
Uriah Heep in the 1970s – Steve Pilkington 978-1-78952-103-0

On Screen series
Carry On… – Stephen Lambe 978-1-78952-004-0
David Cronenberg – Patrick Chapman 978-1-78952-071-2
Doctor Who: The David Tennant Years – Jamie Hailstone 978-1-78952-066-8
Monty Python – Steve Pilkington 978-1-78952-047-7
Seinfeld Seasons 1 to 5 – Stephen Lambe 978-1-78952-012-5

Other Books
Babysitting A Band On The Rocks – G.D. Praetorius 978-1-78952-106-1
Derek Taylor: For Your Radioactive Children – Andrew Darlington 978-1-78952-038-5
Iggy and The Stooges On Stage 1967-1974 – Per Nilsen 978-1-78952-101-6
Jon Anderson and the Warriors – the road to Yes – David Watkinson 978-1-78952-059-0
Nu Metal: A Definitive Guide – Matt Karpe 978-1-78952-063-7
Tommy Bolin: In and Out of Deep Purple – Laura Shenton 978-1-78952-070-5
Maximum Darkness – Deke Leonard 978-1-78952-048-4
Maybe I Should've Stayed In Bed – Deke Leonard 978-1-78952-053-8
The Twang Dynasty – Deke Leonard 978-1-78952-049-1

and many more to come!